A Farewell
TO CHARMS

A
PRINCESS FOR HIRE
BOOK

LINDSEY LEAVITT

Disney • HYPERION BOOKS

NEW YORK

Copyright © 2012 by Lindsey Leavitt

All rights reserved. Published by Disney • Hyperion Books, an imprint of Disney Book Group. No part of this book may be reproduced or transmitted in any form or by any means, electronic or mechanical, including photocopying, recording, or by any information storage and retrieval system, without written permission from the publisher. For information address Disney • Hyperion Books, 114 Fifth Avenue, New York, New York 10011-5690.

First Disney • Hyperion paperback edition, 2013
1 3 5 7 9 10 8 6 4 2
V567-9638-5-11046
Printed in the United States of America

Library of Congress Cataloging-in-Publication for Hardcover: 2011041667
ISBN 978-1-4231-2315-6

Visit www.un-requiredreading.com

To Logan, Princess Charming

Chapter

I

A bead of cold sweat dangled on my fingertip before dripping onto the doorbell. What if I got electrocuted from my wet fingers? I would die literally inches away from my first high school party. And then everyone would be like, oh, poor thing was so nervous, what a tragedy. Death by sweat.

"Come on, Des," said my best friend, Kylee. "It's freezing out here."

Hypothermia *and* electrocution. Just to be safe, I knocked.

The door swung open. A muscular boy with acne and a sour expression leered at me. "Did you just try to ring the doorbell?"

"Uh . . . I knocked, actually," I said.

"No one knocks. What are you, a freshman?"

"We're in eighth grade," Kylee said.

"But *she* helps teach the high school band. She's a musical prodigy," I said.

Kylee punched me on the shoulder. "I hate when you call me a prodigy. I'm just advanced. I mean, musically advanced. It's not like I'm great at everything."

The guy still stood in the doorway, slack-jawed. Was he going to let us in? Was there some secret password we were supposed to say? Did we have to pay an admission fee?

"I'm in the cast," I said.

He blinked.

"For *A Midsummer Night's Dream*. I'm playing the fairy queen. Well, I guess *played*, since tonight was the final night."

"They cut the junior high theater program," Kylee added. "So Desi got to try out and made it—"

"And the assistant director said I could come. Because . . . because I'm in the cast," I finished. Lamely.

"I didn't ask for your résumé, theater freak. You people love to talk, don't you?" He let out a monstrous burp. "I'm crashing the party for the food."

He wandered away, leaving the door open. "Close the door!" someone yelled. "It's November—you want to freeze?"

We rushed inside.

"Great entrance." Kylee tucked a wisp of her black hair

2

behind her ear. "Now we're the clueless, knocking eighth graders."

"I'll make us T-shirts that say that."

We *were* pretty clueless. Everyone in the cast probably thought it was a miracle that I actually got a part in this play. When, really, it wasn't much of a miracle. My work experience as a magical princess substitute meant acting came easily for me.

Yeah, I said magical princess substitute.

Not that anyone knew about my job with the Façade Agency, not even Kylee. The only people aware of my career were the royals I worked for and other Façade employees. The big shocker that I'd just discovered last week was that one of my cast mates, Reed Pearson, was also a substitute for royalty.

Reed was the reason I was here. We needed to finally talk about our magical coincidence. This party provided such a perfect opportunity to be alone that I'd risked the humiliation of having my parents drive me here. I'd insisted that they drop Kylee and me off a block away. My mom waved excitedly out the window while my dad stopped the car one last time to go over who to call in case of an emergency. This was after I'd talked him out of coming inside with us to speak to the parents of the party-thrower. Whoever that was.

I tugged down on my SHAKESPEARE ROCKETH T-shirt, surveying the house's open floor plan. It wasn't like the high school parties I'd seen in movies—no one was swinging from chandeliers, and the furniture was still in place. No

DJ or dancing, either. Everyone was spread out around the house—talking on the couch, eating in the kitchen. The mood resembled parties we had in junior high, except the conversations were more . . . mature. I caught one snippet between two seniors about college applications. *College*.

"So, what are we supposed to do now?" Kylee asked.

"I don't know," I said. "Mingle?"

"There's a horror movie that starts out like this, you know. *Party of the Dead*. These nerdy girls show up at this party that they think is full of popular people, but actually demons possessed all the cool kids' bodies—"

"Coach Kylee!" Steve, a junior who'd played the part of Oberon, slapped Kylee on the back. Steve was nice enough, but he acted like he was on a stage twenty-four/seven. "Did you come to give me a private oboe lesson?"

Kylee's face reddened. "I'm here with Desi. I know it's a cast party, but she didn't want to come alone, so I—"

"I'm glad you came," he said. "Have we ever even talked? Ninety percent of the time we're around each other you're blowing on an instrument. Not the best conversation starter."

Kylee giggled. I thought he might be flirting with her, but I couldn't tell. In junior high, boys still insulted the girls they liked. Or didn't like. It was all very confusing.

"Come on, I'll introduce you to my magical fairy court. You already know my wife, Titania." He pointed at me and lowered his voice. "We're in a little bit of a tiff. She has a crush on a donkey."

4

I rolled my eyes. Always acting.

"He was looking for you, actually," Steve said.

"Who, Reed?" I asked.

"Yeah. He probably wants another smooch." He swung his arm around Kylee. "Go find him. I'm stealing Kylee."

Great. Steve had to bring up the kissing. It was a stage kiss during one solitary performance, and the only reason it had happened was because Reed had misplaced his costume donkey head. And, okay, yes, the kiss was magical, but it wasn't *real*. Reed also gave me mouth-to-mouth last summer when I nearly drowned in a dunk tank, and no one was making snarky comments about *that*.

Kylee's smile faltered. "Oh, so you go talk to Reed, then. Alone, I guess."

"He's probably going to critique my performance tonight." I shrugged. It was a heavy shrug. "He's always doing that."

"Well, tell him I said hi," Kylee said. "And maybe . . . Well, just hi."

"So, do you help the band director with our grades at all?" Steve asked as he guided Kylee outside to a hodgepodge of lawn chairs circling a fire pit.

This Reed thing was going to get sticky. Kylee had liked him since he'd first moved to Idaho last June. We'd spent hours strategizing ways to "run into him," and every time we did, Kylee froze. She'd probably said three sentences to him. Total. She claimed she was going to get over her crush, but it's not that easy. If feelings could be controlled, then I wouldn't like the same guy my best friend liked.

Not that I admitted it to Kylee. And I'd only recently figured out that *Reed* was the boy I liked when I discovered that he worked for Façade and might just be my long-lost Prince Charming. I don't mean that in a cutesy way, either. I'd fallen for Prince Karl while on a job in the Alps, and I'm pretty sure Reed was substituting for him at the time. I still needed to talk to Reed about it, but how could I bring that up? *Hey, Reed, have you ever fallen for a princess while subbing who wasn't really the royal you thought? You have? Yay! That was me! Let's get married! Or at least get a milk shake.*

See? Sticky.

I finally spotted Reed hovering over a bowl of Skittles. He was wearing a fitted gray T-shirt, his olive skin practically glowing in the brightly lit kitchen. It had been two weeks since our stage kiss, followed by two weeks of performances (and two weeks of avoidance, because the weirdness was too much). This moment was the reason I was here, but I couldn't quite convince my feet to move.

Reed looked up, and our eyes locked. And then it didn't matter if I could move or not, because he was already crossing the room. As he walked past our cast mates, they gave him high fives or brayed in honor of his role of Bottom, the donkey. He smiled and laughed, but the whole time he was staring at me.

"Hey," he said, his voice soft. His gaze, so focused on me before, now bounced around the room.

6

I don't know how many times we'd said *hey* or *hello* or *hi* during rehearsals. I couldn't count them, because they hadn't mattered. But now everything seemed to matter—his hair, his mouth, and the way his New Zealand accent managed to make the word "hey" sound beautiful. He was the same, but totally new.

I smiled. "Hey."

He held up his arms like he was displaying something to the left of him. "What do you think?"

I blinked at the blank space. "What do I think about what?"

"This lovely elephant in the room." Reed pretended to pet the air. "What should we name him? Something like e-way are-way oth-bay oyal-ray ubs-say?"

Pig Latin. *We are both royal subs*. Yeah, it was the elephant between us—the truth that we hadn't yet been able to discuss—but the funny thing was that we were the only ones at this party aware of our secret.

"I thought we weren't supposed to talk about . . . where we work." I glanced around the party, worried that my agent, Meredith, was going to pop out of her traveling bubble at any moment. "Faça . . . I mean, our boss watches us, you know."

Reed patted his fake pet. "You know what's great about invisible elephants? They're easy to make disappear. Come on."

He grabbed my hand, and we dodged through the guests. My first high school party and I was already holding a guy's hand! Who, okay, was only leading me away so we could discuss magic, but it still gave me a thrill. Part of me thought to let go, in case Kylee saw, but my fingers wouldn't listen to that rational part of my brain. Fingers are tricky like that.

Reed pounded on the door of a bathroom and led me inside.

"Don't tell me we're giving the elephant a bath now," I said.

Reed hit some buttons on his manual, a small touch-screen computer that had all the information we needed about the agency and our clients. He was using this device when I'd first put together his connection to Façade.

"I need yours," Reed said.

When he was done punching keys on my manual, he blew air through his nose. "No interruptions—I muted Central Command's surveillance on us. Anytime we're together with our manuals now, it'll block out our conversation. Just try not to look suspicious so they zoom in to lip-read when they figure out there isn't any noise."

"You can do that?"

"Little technical loophole I picked up along the way. There are all sorts of hidden applications on here. I just downloaded a key system that allows me access to anywhere in our Specter offices—I'm sure you could find one for Façade, too. And I've heard about some sort of scanner you can use to check if a royal is real or a sub. Haven't figured that one out yet."

"Yeah, but . . . does Façade care? Those kind of applications give the subs too much power."

8

"The agency put the apps on the phone. Of course we can use them. Besides"—he gave me a funny look—"we're employees, not fugitives. We still have the right to privacy."

I wasn't so sure about that. Façade did some questionable things to hopeful employees who didn't meet their standards. During my last agency visit, I'd found the sub-sanitation room, the place where potential subs' magic was unknowingly stripped and stored for Façade purposes. I had no clue how many people had endured this treatment, or if there were dangerous side effects. I didn't know what to do with the information—if I should keep quiet or try to stop Façade. I hoped Reed would help me find the courage to decide what to do. I just had to open up to him first.

"They can still see us," I whispered.

"If they're watching. The sub security device Façade uses is a roving radar. And they have much more important things to do than watch two subs talking about elephants at a cast party."

"But, say they *are* watching, shouldn't we be somewhere less suspicious? Like out there, eating Skittles, instead of in a bathroom? They're less likely to watch if we're acting normal."

"True. Wow, you're really paranoid."

Reed would be paranoid too if he knew what I knew about Façade. "Professional. Not paranoid."

"I thought it'd be nice if we could . . . be alone," Reed said. "I mean, to talk." We both didn't say anything for a bit. The silence was awkward but exhilarating. Reed wanted to

9

be alone with me! Even if it was in a small bathroom with peeling floral wallpaper. He eased onto the edge of the bathtub and motioned to the toilet seat. "Now I finally have you here, and we're safe. So sit. And tell me everything."

Chapter
2

I ran my fingers over the mauve toilet seat cover. Who invented those things, anyway? You can't really fancify a toilet. I reached over and rinsed off my hands in the sink. Bleh. "Okay. So what part of the elephant should we talk about first? Heads or tails?"

"Your choice," Reed said. "You can tell me when you started working for Façade, or we could finally talk about what happened opening night—"

"Heads it is." I wasn't ready to talk about that kiss. What do you say? *Yep. We kissed. It was great. Fantastic.* But I also cared about my best friend's feelings. And what if that kiss with Reed was only great because we were both magical, and what if Reed didn't like me like I thought I liked him, and I really shouldn't be liking anyone right now anyway when there was the world's magical population to worry about?

Better to start at the beginning. As one of my favorite actresses, Julie Andrews, said in the classic musical *The Sound of Music*—that's a very good place to start. I ran my tongue along my braces. "So I used to work at the mall pet store, Pets Charming—"

The words came slowly while I tried to piece my history together. But then I got going. I told Reed all about my background—about the wish on a magical fish that ignited my MP (Magic Potential), about Meredith, about my first trip to the Court of Royal Appeals, and my advancement to Level Two.

I didn't tell him the big thing we needed to discuss—whether or not he knew that Façade was run on stolen magic. I'd only found out the truth by accident, and the head of Façade, Genevieve, claimed that stripping magic and washing the subs' Façade memories was in everyone's best interest. I'd tried to push aside all my nagging doubts over the past couple of weeks, but ignoring a secret like this was like finding out all the food in the school cafeteria was secretly pig's vomit and then still eating it. Those poor subs never had a chance to realize their possibilities. Façade even called the power MP—Magic Potential—and yet the potential part was taken away if the sub wasn't of use to Façade.

See? The news was so big that I had to find a way to ease into it. But there was something so trusting about the way Reed was leaning in, listening to my every word.

Trusting, and very cute.

"So how long have you been home?" he asked, once I finished sharing Desi's Career with Façade: The Edited Version.

"I'd just come back from my last job when the play started. Not long."

"All of that and you've only been there since June? Huh." He was still leaning toward me, and I caught a whiff of his sporty cologne—or soap or laundry detergent or whatever it was that made him smell so good—and realized that we were very close in a very small space. Our knees were practically touching. Did he notice that? Did he think about how I smelled and that it was different than usual because I'd spritzed on some of my mom's perfume before coming to the party? Because . . . well, because I knew Reed would be here.

"What about you?" I asked, my voice hoarse.

"I've been with Specter longer." Specter was a newer branch of Façade, specializing in male royalty. Façade was originally female only, so there was a bit of a rivalry between the subbing branches of Façade and Specter. So although Reed officially worked under Façade, it was easy for us to never run into each other with our offices located in different countries.

"How long?" I asked.

"I signed on right when I turned thirteen, so two years, now."

"How many times have you subbed?"

"Sixty-five jobs and counting."

"What? But you've only been with them two years—"

"But with the Law of Duplicity, it's been much longer."

"Yeah, I guess technically you could work hundreds of jobs without missing anything at home. You must have big client demand." Meredith once described the Law of Duplicity like this: the time we're on a job is like a piece of string stretched out. The magic has the power to bring those string tips together again, like the time away never happened, returning us home seconds after we left. I mean, it's more technical than that, of course, but that's the gist. People at Façade also seemed to age slower, but that might have something to do with their extensive magical makeup line.

"It's a good schedule," Reed said. "If you break it down over two years, that's really only one job every week or two."

"Still," I said. "You must be really good if they're sending you out that much."

"I do what I do." He smiled ruefully. "It doesn't hurt that my parents were both subs. I'm a legacy."

Façade had legacies? That sounded like a big deal. And if Reed was a big deal, then maybe he knew more cool tricks beyond manipulating manuals. Then again, maybe he already knew everything there was to know about Façade and still thought things were fabulous. "But I thought magic wasn't hereditary."

"It isn't always. But it can be. And in my case, it was." Reed glanced around the bathroom before lowering his voice.

Even in this space, even when our words were supposedly muted, I could tell it was hard for him to talk about Façade too. "Part of the reason my parents work in agriculture and move around so much is because they're doing research for the agency. They work for the Organic Magic department, figuring out which organic things house magic. So I actually already knew about your pet-store fish—we've been tracking them since we moved to Sproutville. Along with dozens of other organisms—it's a hot pocket of activity. Who'd have thought Idaho would be so magical?"

Not me. I pulled my legs up to my chest and rested my chin on my knees. "So did you always have magic, or did you have to have it . . . ignited?"

"Same rules. My ignition happened with a seal at the zoo. It was pretty staged—my parents paid the seal trainer fifty bucks to pick me during the animal show. But I was still nervous that nothing would happen, that I didn't have MP. And everyone's ignition is different—some people don't even know anything happened, and others have a big magical explosion. Kind of depends on how your magic shows itself and what your talents are."

"So? What happened to you?"

"My mom says the water literally glowed when I touched the seal."

"Wow. I had a stupid fish blow bubbles."

"It's all relative," Reed said. "I went into the family business right away. The second we got home, I was out the door and off to work."

"And do you like working at Façade?" I searched his face as I spoke, hoping for a little hesitation.

"Don't you?" Reed asked. "I bet you love wearing all those tiaras."

I snorted. "I still haven't worn a tiara! That's something I would change—every sub should get her own tiara."

"Very important," Reed agreed.

"What about you?" I nudged his knee, hoping we could go deeper. "Would you change anything?"

Reed looked up at the ceiling. "Um, no? It's the most fantastic job known to man. Or woman. Don't you think?"

I shrugged. If Reed thought everything was peachy, he obviously didn't know about the poor subs who had their memory washed and magic stolen. If he did, would he still think it's the best job ever? Or would he team up with me so together we could . . . what? Take over the magical world? "Reed. I have something I should tell you—"

There was a knock on the door. I guess door-knocking at a high school party is approved for bathrooms, just not front doors. Noted. "Hey, whoever is in there, you need to hurry. There's a line."

I cringed. Reed could block Façade, but not the one other eighth grader in the cast. Celeste Juniper, my ex-best friend. Former enemy. And now, since I'd helped her win second runner-up at Miss Teen Dream Idaho she was . . . a frenemy? Still, I did *not* need her walking in while Reed and I were talking in the bathroom. Who knew what rumor she would start.

Reed jerked his head toward the tub and whispered, "Get in."

I did, soundlessly. He closed the shower curtain behind me. I crouched down and watched through the little slit between the curtain and tile.

Reed cracked the door open. "Hi, Celeste. Where's the fire?"

Celeste's voice turned to syrup. "Reed! I didn't know you were in there."

"Yeah, and I don't see this line you were worried about."

Celeste giggled. "If you don't make things urgent, people don't listen."

"Well, I was just making an *urgent* phone call." Reed held up his cell phone for added effect. "And I need privacy. So would you mind finding another loo? Please?"

"Loo! I love your Englandy words."

"I'm from New Zealand."

"Same thing." She pouted her lips. "I just need to check my makeup. What do you think? Do I look all right?"

I swallowed a laugh. Watching Celeste flirt without any reciprocation was awesome.

A ringing interrupted my thoughts. Oh. My phone was ringing. Wait, let me rephrase that. MY PHONE WAS RINGING. I ripped it out of my pocket and tried to turn off my cell, but you can't unring a ring.

Celeste peeked behind Reed. "Is someone else in there?"

"Nope. Just me."

"But that was a phone. In the shower. And you're already holding your phone."

Either the girl had superhuman strength or she caught Reed by surprise, because she pushed past him and opened the shower curtain. I waved feebly.

"Desi? What are you . . . Oh, my gosh . . . Were you two—"

"No!" Reed and I shouted in unison.

"We were just talking," I said.

"About . . . about the play. And, er . . ." Reed shot me a lost look.

"Shakespeare's comedies!" I added. "He was great at writing misunderstood situations. Just like this."

Celeste wrinkled her nose. "You were talking about Shakespeare. In the bathroom."

We nodded.

"What you two want to do together is *your* business." Celeste placed her hand over her heart. "You don't have to worry. I won't tell a *soul* that you were in here. I'm just going to find another bathroom now so you two can . . . be alone."

She skipped away. Not good. I laid my head down on the side of the tub.

"What do you think she's going to tell everyone?" Reed asked.

I raised my head. "Probably that we got married and have three kids."

Reed's expression turned thoughtful. "I always wanted four children, if that's all right. Perhaps twins, if you can arrange it."

He was joking, of course, but . . . I still had a little happy jolt. Twins! I would dress them in matching overalls whenever we helped Reed's parents on the farm. I wondered if our kids would be magical, too, what kind of zany adventures the old Pearson family would have—

"So, what should we do?" Reed asked.

"What? Oh." I scrambled out of the tub. "I better call Kylee before Celeste finds her. Hold on a second."

Kylee answered on the third ring. "There you are. I just tried calling you."

"Yeah, sorry." And thanks for calling at *exactly* that moment. Spot-on timing, my friend. "Did you finish your private lesson with Oberon?"

"Gah!" Kylee exclaimed. "That guy is such a flirt."

"He's never flirted with me, and we're married."

"Where are you?" she asked.

Oh. I should have come up with a battle plan before calling. All that talk of twins muddled my head. (Would they have Reed's skin color? I hope so. I burn easily, and I wouldn't want to have to worry about sunscreen every time we went to the beach in New Zealand.)

How long had Reed and I been in there talking? Half an hour? Even if it was five minutes, Kylee was going to grill me on our conversation. I didn't think she would buy the Shakespeare comedies line, either. "Oh, I ran into Reed."

"Really? Seriously, where are you? I've been all over the house."

I stood. "Um, in the bathroom."

"You ran into Reed in the bathroom?" Kylee asked.

"No. Well, sort of. Nothing embarrassing. He was, er, washing his hands. So we talked for a second." I slapped my forehead. I was awful at this. "Just go to the kitchen. I'll meet you there."

I hung up the phone. "Reed. I know this is kind of a weird request, but can you, um, stay away from me? For the rest of the party? It's just, I have to go talk to Kylee, and I don't know how to act around you when she's there. It's been hard enough covering up my own magic from her, but she's going to figure out that there's more between us now."

Reed raised his eyebrows. "More between us?"

"I mean, MAGIC. We both have it. And Façade. So, you know, it's a connection. A work connection. We're colleagues."

"Colleagues." Reed moved his jaw, like he was chewing on the word. "Okay. But don't worry about magic. I've covered it up my whole life. I'm a master of mystery."

"Well, keep up that disguise anytime the three of us are together. Things should be just how they were before."

"Right. How they were before." Reed leaned over the sink and washed his hands. "But can we meet up again? Later? There are other things we need to talk about."

"Sure." I was halfway down the hallway when something occurred to me. Did he mean other things about Façade? Or other things about . . . about us?

Chapter
3

For the first time in my life, I was glad to have a ten o'clock weekend curfew. Well, not a curfew, exactly. My dad still used the word *bedtime*.

Dad picked up Kylee and me around the corner from the house. She didn't bring up Reed. I think she was waiting for me to, and there was no way I was going to talk about *that* elephant. So we talked about the party food the whole way to Kylee's house. When we pulled into her driveway, my dad looked at us in his rearview mirror.

"I'm glad you girls had fun at the party and didn't, I don't know, swing from chandeliers. But next time you might want to branch away from the chips and dip."

"Thanks, Mr. Bascomb." Kylee unclicked her seat belt and turned to me. "Hey, Des? Can we talk for a second? Outside?"

My dad fiddled with the radio dial. "Go ahead. I'll just listen to my music while you discuss the different pizza toppings."

Kylee and I slid out of the car and sat down on the curb. My dad was playing this old band called Bon Jovi and air-guitaring. "Do you think he was born a dork, or is that something you develop?" I asked Kylee.

"It's genetic. Look at you."

"Funny."

She twirled the tip of her braid. "So, you're killing me. Tell me what happened. You ran into Reed in the bathroom, and then what?"

"I told you. We talked for a bit."

"What about?"

I yanked a weed from a crack in the sidewalk. Our magical employer. Same old. "Play stuff."

"Did you talk about Reed losing his donkey head?"

You mean did we talk about kissing? "Kylee, why do you have to grill me every time I talk to Reed? It was a regular old conversation, just like any other conversation I've had with him."

She dropped her braid. "I don't get the same chances to talk to him."

"That's because you never create opportunities."

"So, did I come up?"

"No." I tried to keep the edge out of my voice, but I swear we'd had this talk a million times. It was mildly annoying before, but now this just plain sucked. What was I supposed to say to her? Yes, we liked the same boy, but I didn't *know* he was the same boy when I started to like him, because he *wasn't* the same boy at the time—he was a prince. I'd spent months thinking I liked Prince Karl, when all the wonderful things about him were really Reed pretending to be Karl. And I would tell her this, but if I did, I'd get fired. And maybe lose my magic.

Oh, yeah. P.S., I have magic.

"Okay," she said. "Jeez. Sorry."

Here's the thing about having magic: everyone has an emotion or trait that allows him or her to tune into his or her power. Mine's empathy, so when I emotionally relate and connect to my clients, I'm able to channel my magic to help them. And that ability to magically serve isn't exclusive to royals, despite what Façade would have its employees believe. *Anyone* could benefit from my magic, if I could just figure out what, exactly, I was capable of doing. So far, I'd managed to conjure up an agency bubble, talk to Celeste with my mind, and figure out what a lot of princesses wanted. But I had yet to come up with a concrete way to use my powers in real life.

Right now would be a really good time for some magic. But it's not like I could shoot a love potion out of my finger so that Kylee liked some other boy and our problem disappeared. It didn't work like that.

Wait. Unless it did! I had no idea what I was able to do

using my magical emotion. Maybe I *could* clear this all up with a little cupid action.

I squeezed my eyes shut and concentrated on my supportive, sweet best friend and her crush on Reed and all her needs and feelings and problems and hopes. I pictured the perfect boy for her—someone funny and smart and talented and cute and NOT REED. I knew Kylee so well; it wasn't hard to get my empathy pumping. Then I pointed, willing all my power to pool into my fingertip. Crush be gone. Alacazam!

"Des? Why are you pointing at me?"

I opened one eye. "Do you feel . . . anything special when I do that?"

"Do what?"

"Point?"

"Besides weirded out? No."

I dropped my hand. Stupid Cupid.

"What, are you trying to put a hex on me so I'll stop asking about Reed?" Kylee's eyes lit up. "I saw that in this teen horror movie, *Planet Hex*, where this girl had a wand inserted into her fingernail, but it was controlled by an alien from this alternate *galaxy*—"

I sighed while Kylee rambled on about the flick. My magic powers were a bust, but at least I deflected her questioning by reminding her of another scary movie.

"—but then she ended up *liking* the alien, so it all worked out."

"Mmm hmm," I said.

"So, anyway." Kylee flicked a rock in the gutter. "Did Reed ask you to the Winter Ball when you were in the bathroom?"

"What are you talking about?" Sproutville's Winter Ball was a huge festival with ice skating, hot chocolate, snowy sleigh rides, games, and yes . . . a "ball," which was really just the community center jazzed up with decorations and a cheesy DJ. There weren't many chances for girls my age to dance with boys, so they got all dressed up and pretended the "ball" was something fancier than it was. "Reed and I aren't going together," I said. "Don't be ridiculous."

Kylee didn't look at me when she spoke. "The only thing ridiculous is that you're keeping something from your best friend."

"I'm not." I rubbed my forehead. "Seriously, I told you that Reed and I—"

"I know you, Des. I know when you're nervous. I know when you're lying. And things have been different ever since the play started. It's like sometimes . . . you're someone else, thinking about some other world. And you don't tell me *anything* anymore."

I started to interrupt, but Kylee held up a hand. "Don't deny it. And it's like, it's like Reed knows you better than me, even though you only saw each other at rehearsal. *You're* different around *him*."

"Kylee! Listen, you are my very best friend and I tell you absolutely everything I can."

"Everything you *can*. But not everything." She shook

her head. "And that's what hurts the most. More than the fact that we like the same boy and I think he likes you. I can get over that eventually. It's a crush, not undying vampire love. I was already getting used to the fact that I would never be able to talk to him. But I think he knows what's up with you. You've told him, but you won't tell me."

I didn't say anything. I *couldn't* say anything. She was right. About all of it. And it blew my mind that Kylee knew me so well, that she was perceptive enough to know that I had a huge secret. It was just a much different secret than she thought.

Kylee stood up and brushed off her jeans. "Sorry, that's been on my mind for a while. I guess the party just brought it out. I'm going inside."

"Yeah, I better go before someone from the party walks by and sees my dad head-banging in his car," I said. "Can we talk more? Tomorrow?"

"Maybe next week. I need some time to, um, think." Kylee gave me a weak smile before running up her driveway and disappearing into her house.

Whew. I didn't have many solutions here. I had to either tell her the truth about Reed and Façade, or get my magic to fix everything. Otherwise, our friendship was going to take a serious hit. And it's not like there are a million Kylees running around Idaho, or even the world. Or even this galaxy.

While Kylee was probably home watching something dumb like *My Best Friend Was Abducted by an Alien*, I put on

Casablanca, a movie I had always adored but now watched with special attention. Right before our play had started, Reed quoted a line from this movie. And my princely crush, Karl, said the same lines the first time I met him. Karl later claimed he hadn't even heard of *Casablanca*. So how many freshman boys know lines from a seventy-year-old movie and use them in conversation? Reed *had* to be Karl's sub. He had to.

The movie ended, and the music from the credits was interrupted by a familiar vibrating sound from inside my purse. My manual. Wait, my manual? Now?

So much for a quiet night at home.

Darling,

I hope this finds you well. I snuck into your final performance and saw you kiss that poor boy's costume head. I hope it was dry-cleaned regularly. But, brava! So much spirit and talent. So strange that you would be cast alongside another employee of Façade, and a rather valuable one at that.

Yes, we know about Reed Pearson. Of course we know. Although a relationship between subs is permissible, it's not promoted. We don't want you comparing circumstances—it's important to remember every sub has a different experience. You are all special to the agency. So although we certainly won't forbid you from remaining friends with Mr. Pearson now that you're aware of your commonalities, we do hope you keep your interactions light.

Focus on adolescent concerns, whatever those may be. No plotting to take over the greatest magical organization in the world. Ha!

In other news, preparations have already begun for my promotion to the Façade council. Such a delicious secret I've been carrying around—the news will be announced at an upcoming formal ceremony. What to wear, what to wear? While I consider that, you should get started on your next gig. Yes, I've included your Betterment of Elite Sub Training, better known as BEST. Although BEST is still considered part of Level Two, we've never had a sub rise so suddenly, and we're still making arrangements for your promotion. Usually, a match is selected after a sub has worked for a particular client many times over many years. So we'd like you to do this job while we finalize your long-term position.

And don't worry. This list might seem daunting, but now that you're so in tune with your magical emotion, we know you'll shine in any position! Empathy can be felt for the strongest or feeblest of princesses, and once you get going, your magic will take care of the rest. Mastery of this BEST list would be impossible, so do what you are able. Further information on this particular princess will be available once we feel you're prepared for the task. Which should be soon. You've had your time to play, now it's time for work.

Ta-ta,

Meredith

Betterment of Elite Sub Training

1. Gymnastics
2. Coding and advanced computer technology
3. Lock-picking
4. Fencing
5. Karate
6. Sculpture
7. Build up a tolerance to pain
8. Stealth

I shook my manual a couple times. Somehow, I'd been sent a list for a ninja movie action hero, not a princess. But the words didn't budge. This was legit.

At least I knew how to use my magic when I was subbing. I literally put myself in my client's shoes and intuitively knew what they wanted or needed. And I was going to need all the help I could get because . . . Building up a tolerance to pain? That has to be breaking some employment laws right there. And it's not like they had stuntwoman training in Idaho. Not to mention *gymnastics*. Given my inability to do a somersault, the outlook was not good.

As always, I had no clue when Meredith would be back. The BEST list was created to prepare me for my next job, and in the past I'd had weeks, even months, of research before beginning the gig. Quality over quantity, Meredith said. But that obviously wasn't the case anymore. They wanted me, and they wanted me soon.

What they wanted me to do, I still couldn't say. But

I had a feeling this job was not going to involve a ball gown.

I spent the rest of my weekend preparing for my BEST by watching old ninja movies and fiddling with a homemade lock-picking kit I had read about. As far as building up a tolerance to pain, I'd once heard that my favorite actress, screen legend Audrey Hepburn, used to pluck her nose hairs when she needed to cry in a movie. And yeah, the exercise brought tears to my eyes. I just hoped my biggest casualty was losing nose hairs, not major body parts.

I didn't do any more research beyond that. I could have done a search on karate/fencing/gymnastic princesses in the sub chat room and figured out my client's name. Really, how many princesses fit that BEST description? But I needed more time to talk to Reed before I went back to work. I wasn't ready for Façade just yet.

Then again, I wasn't really prepared for school on Monday either.

It started in homeroom when Celeste's boyfriend, Hayden Garrison, leaned over and whispered, "So how long have you been going out with that guy from New Zealand?"

Why was Hayden Garrison talking to me? He never talked to me—the kid still thought my name was Daisy. Six months ago, when I still had a stupid crush on the guy, I would have danced with glee. Now I just stared at him blankly.

"Huh?"

"Celeste told me you were going out with . . . What's his name?"

"You mean, Reed?"

"Yeah. I heard he's sixteen."

I jerked back. "He's not sixteen. And no! I'm not going out with him."

"Oh." Hayden shrugged. "'Kay. Just asking."

And for the next three periods, the popular people noticed me, asked me the same thing or even crazier versions—*So, I heard you're skipping a grade next year so you two can have all the same classes together*. Which meant that Kylee had heard these same rumors. One look at her in the lunch line confirmed this.

Even a magical love potion couldn't help the rift in our friendship now. If she thought I was keeping things from her before, rumors of my supposed "relationship" with Reed had sent Kylee over the edge.

She didn't even make eye contact with me, just ran right out of the cafeteria. I followed after her, tripping on a stray backpack. She wasn't there when I got to the main hallway. My skin tingled with empathy, and I closed my eyes hoping that some magical solution would come. How could I fix this?

A little voice in the back of my head whispered: *Go tell her about your magic*.

Oh, yeah. Truth. That would help. She'd totally believe that. I'm sure Façade would love that, too. I squeezed my eyes even tighter and asked myself, my magic, again. What do I do?

Give her a hug.

I kicked a nearby locker. Seriously, magic. A hug? A HUG? Unless you're a cuddly woodland creature in a cheery musical cartoon, a hug doesn't fix anything. Thanks for nothing.

This double-life thing was really starting to suck.

Chapter
4

Kylee ran away from me when I tried to talk to her during last period, and of course she didn't answer any of my zillion calls or texts. So after school, I ordered her a fruit basket online. I couldn't tell her my secrets, but at least I could give the girl some pears.

The sooner I figured out what I wanted to do with Façade, the sooner I could master my magic, which hopefully wouldn't feed me any more "hugging" garbage. So I made another phone call, one that I was almost dreading more than convincing Kylee that all was well.

"Hi, Reed. How are you? It's Desi Bascomb."

"Hi, Desi Bascomb, also known as the only Desi I know."

"Just wanted to make sure."

"And I know your voice. And I have caller ID—"

I rolled my eyes. He could be so aggravating sometimes. "Are you criticizing my *greeting* now?"

"Sorry. Hi."

I took a breath. "So I'm calling to talk about—"

"Hey, why don't you come over?"

"Oh, um, that's okay." A boy's house? No way would my parents let that happen. Not to mention, I mean, I can't go to his house! Way too weird. "We can just talk now. You know, about—"

"Elephants. I know. But it's probably better *in person*."

And then I understood. Reed didn't think it was safe for us to talk over the phone. In person we could mute ourselves. It was the first time I had the courage to call a boy, and we couldn't talk because our magical employer might hear us.

"Oh. Yeah. Elephants. I have a lot of questions about those."

"So why don't you come with me to work?"

"The roller-skating rink?" I asked. "Will they let me?"

"Sure. I'm supposed to start getting stuff together for some big event next month. You can help me. It's your civic duty."

Civic duty. Civic duties were parent approved. "Great, I'll meet you at Crystal Palace, then."

"I'll see you in fifteen minutes."

Fifteen minutes sounded reasonable enough, but nothing was reasonable when it came to my dad. He'd come home early to help with my little sister, Gracie, since my mom wasn't feeling well. Again. Truthfully, I thought she was overworking herself with all her pageant consultations. Ever since Celeste had placed second runner-up, her schedule was packed and her energy level seemed way down. She probably needed to eat better—she skipped dinner a lot and ate ice cream instead. And as much as I loved my dad and as nice as it was to spend time with him, everything was a little more . . . labor intensive when he was around.

It took half an hour to get over to the skating rink, because we had to wait until Gracie woke up from her nap. Then my dad had to pack a diaper bag, even though he wasn't getting out of the car. Then he had to load a grumpy Gracie into her car seat. Then he drove four miles an hour on a thirty-five mph road.

"Dad, have you ever heard the expression 'put the pedal to the metal'?" I asked.

"All the time. It's what people do before they get into car accidents."

"Arghh."

"Look, we're here. And, hey, I like the shirt."

I smiled down at the new print on my purple thermal— ON A ROLL with a little blue roller skate. I hoped Reed appreciated it too. I was kind of second-guessing making a shirt that was just for his entertainment.

Dad cleared his throat. "Actually, Princess, I wanted to ask you something."

I unclicked my seat belt. "Yeah?"

"Is everything all right?"

Why was everyone always asking me that? "Sure."

"Good. It's just that . . . Mom found a lock-picking kit in your room."

I froze. Why hadn't I hidden that? At least she didn't find my manual. "That wouldn't happen if she wasn't so crazy about cleaning. You'd think with her being so tired, she could cut back on her vacuum rampages."

Dad snorted. "Mom's not tired."

"She's napping right now."

"Oh." He cut me a look. "You noticed."

"Yeah, I'm quick like that." Why'd he act like a nap was something scandalous? I'd be tired too if I was a mom and doing all those pageants and going Mrs. Clean on our house all day. "So I appreciate it, but maybe she could nap more and leave my stuff alone."

"True, but . . . do I need to worry about you? You aren't"—he laughed softly. Nervously—"turning to a life of crime, are you?"

"No, I'm just sharpening my Girl Scout skills."

"But you were never *in* Girl Scouts."

Life of crime. He was so far off, and yet so right. I leaned over the seat and pecked him on the cheek. "Don't worry, Dad. Whatever it is I'm doing, I'm very well paid."

I shut the door and ran over to the back of Crystal Palace. Reed's tandem bike was propped up against the wall. I couldn't believe he was biking in this cool weather. I gave his horn a little honk. He poked his head out and grinned.

"Took you long enough. Awesome shirt, by the way."

I was going to wear this shirt every day for the rest of my life. And, wow. Reed had a nice smile. Was his smile always that nice? And why couldn't I tone down my own goofy grin around him? This was highly unprofessional.

I followed him inside. The skating rink was empty, but music was playing and the disco ball was turning. "It's senior citizen skate day." Reed shook his head. "I keep telling the owner, Chuck, that it's a bad idea. No one ever shows. But it means I have some extra time to get things going for this event. Come on."

I expected a room filled with colorful balloons and crepe paper, but the large party room was packed with shoe boxes. I removed a lid, and another. Ice skates. "Wait," I said, my heart sinking. "What party is this?"

"Some festival happening next month. Chuck is one of the organizers, so we run the ice-skating rink. I've got to clean all the skates, check the laces, that kind of stuff. And we have to decorate the ticket booth, and Chuck's sister is on the decorations committee so he also volunteered me for that. It's still a month away, but with Thanksgiving next week and Christmas stuff, he wants us to get as much done as we can. It must be *some* party."

"It's the Winter Ball," I said.

"Please tell me you did not just make that up. This town has a *ball?*"

"You've lived in Sproutville for five months now, Reed. Why does this surprise you?"

"I don't know. I've been to galas and balls all around the world, just never thought I'd have the opportunity to attend one in Sproutville."

"You were right before—it's more like a festival with a dance attached." I swung my leg over the side of the picnic table and started unlacing a skate. "They do snow sculptures in the park next to the community center, and the madrigal group sings with a band. There's a forest decorated with lights, the school kids make snowflakes, and there's punch and—"

"Punch? Red or pink?"

"Don't make fun." For all its quirks, Sproutville was my home. It was okay if I found fault with it, but Reed was still a newcomer, a very well-traveled newcomer, and I imagined he looked at this place like the Podunk capital of the world. "It's tradition. Everyone in town dresses up, there's glitter and snow, and it's pretty magical."

"Why do they dress up?"

"Oh, for the dance."

"Are you going?" he asked.

He wasn't asking if I was going because he wanted me to go with him. He was making small talk. Wasn't he? "Like I said, everyone goes."

"Huh."

Want to know what I wished my special emotion was? Mind reading. Even selective, Reed-mind reading would be great.

"It does sound cool." He slid next to me on the bench.

Not super close. Maybe two feet away close. Not that I was mentally measuring the distance. "But you know what I don't get? Why does everyone think glitter equals magic? Do you know how much glitter we have at Specter? Zip. It's the second most magical building in the world after Façade, and the only thing you'll see twinkling there is the gold."

"What *is* Specter like?" I tucked my knees under my chin, grateful for the subject change.

"It's in London—a big time boys' club. Not football games and potato chips; more like expensive gadgets and open space and power. I imagine Façade is different."

"You haven't been there?" I asked. "But you've been working for them for so long."

"Specter has everything subs need to perform, so there was never a reason to go to the main office. I was actually invited to Genevieve's costume party, but that was our play's opening night, and it felt like too much to manage."

"I went. Sort of. I mean, I was at Façade that night. But for other reasons." Other reasons being Meredith took me to the sub-sanitation room to see colorful canisters of stolen, synthesized magic. In case you didn't hear about that. "Specter was there, actually, doing all these games."

"Yeah. Big rivalry. Did you know they didn't have guy subs until the Victorian era because they were worried that men would be less noble with the power? So the women run the show. I think some of the guys look at the competitions as a chance to show their manliness."

"They had a pie-eating contest."

"I know. I trained for months for that. I even tried rhubarb."

I made a face. "I didn't even know Specter existed until I figured you out."

"Figured me out when you snuck up on me."

"You were the one with your manual in plain view."

Reed wiggled his eyebrows. "You consider a male dressing room plain view?"

Something crashed in the rink. We both startled. Reed recovered first and stuck his head out the door. "Hello?" When no one answered, he slipped into the darkness in pursuit of the noise.

I hugged myself. Meredith's little note attached to my BEST list made me nervous that Façade was watching, and I didn't want anyone interrupting us right now. I needed to tell Reed about the sub-sanitation room, and then I needed him to help me come up with a clear plan.

Reed shrugged when he came back. "I didn't see anyone. Hope no one was trying to get in."

"Maybe a bubble crashed back there."

"We better stay low, then." Reed pushed some boxes over and sat down on the table. "This is so weird that you even know about bubbles. I've never talked to anyone about my job before. I have my parents, but it's been so long since they subbed."

"At least you have them," I flipped open a shoe box and started relacing another skate. "I feel like I'm living a double life. Kylee went off on me today because she thinks we have a secret, which we do, and then there were the rumors—"

"What rumors?"

"Oh." Of course he wouldn't know. Celeste had spread the gossip at *my* school, but Reed was in high school. "Nothing."

"Did it have something to do with the party?" Reed's expression was bemused. "Did she give us three kids or four?"

"Shut up. Bathroom bonding is big stuff in junior high."

"What did you say to everyone?" Reed asked.

"What do you mean?"

"You know what I mean." Reed stared at me with a gaze so intense I could swear his magical talent was X-ray vision.

"Just . . . the truth. At least the part of the truth I could say." I looked down. I couldn't handle him when he looked at me like that. "That we were just friends talking."

I'd missed one of the holes and had to undo the laces. I yanked at them furiously, relieved I had a task to focus on, when Reed gently bent down and whispered in my ear.

"I think we have different definitions of the truth."

Did that mean we weren't "just" talking since the conversation was about Façade, or did he mean that he thought we were more than "just" friends? And did it matter, either way? It's not like we could ever be more, not with Kylee and Façade. I exhaled. He was so close, I could hear him breathing. I could *feel* him breathing. And when I was this close to him, the air became so heavy with magic that I could hardly breathe.

There was a jolt in my side, just like the first time I ever saw Reed, just like when he pulled me out of the dunk tank, just like when we held hands couple-skating, and just like when we stage-kissed.

"Manual," he said in a low voice.

"What?"

"Your manual just went off." He patted his pockets. "Didn't you feel that jolt? Mine, too."

Oh. Okay. The manual made the jolt. Of course.

I fumbled in my purse, which was so old lady, but I had to carry my Façade stuff in something. My manual was indeed dinging, and I almost threw it, partially to make it stop, but mostly because of the interruption.

"'Be there in ten minutes.' Oh, great," I said.

"Mine says it's urgent," Reed looked puzzled. "There isn't anything on my schedule, and my agent, Sergei, never picks me up anymore. I wonder what's going on."

I shook my head. Time to stay focused—no more thinking about Reed in any way other than as a necessary ally. Because I was running out of time. In a few more minutes, Meredith would whisk me away to a job I hadn't properly prepared for, and who knew when Reed and I would get another opportunity to talk.

Now was the time to tell my secret.

"Are we still muted?" I asked. "They can't hear us?"

"Not as long as we both have our manual settings still on. Why? Did you get the same note on your manual today that I did?"

"Where they didn't forbid our friendship." Actually,

the word was "relationship," but I wasn't going to use that.

"But they weren't going to encourage it. Yeah, something like that." Reed fiddled with the buttons on his manual. "So I've been thinking about this since the other night. Here's my solution: the agency knows we're friends, and they knew that before we even figured out the magic thing. And we're just talking about work—same thing you do in the sub chat rooms, but in person. That note is really just their way of telling us that they aren't going to make us best-friend bracelets, but it's fine. Let's just not start a mutiny." He laughed.

I swallowed. Mutiny. Meredith once told me, right before my hearing with the Court of Royal Appeals, that there were all sorts of punishments Façade enforced in the past for employees who made mistakes. Those mistakes weren't always big—Façade did not mess around.

But I didn't want a mutiny—I just wanted to fix the sub-sanitizing part. Façade did so much good. Subbing for princesses gave me a chance to make an impact in their lives, and the lives of the people they touched. Happy royals equals happy subjects, even if royalty didn't directly rule people like they used to. In short, I was still helping someone, and making a load of money doing it. And there was the glamour and mystery and luxury and fun of working for Façade. And tiaras! Dang it, I STILL WANTED MY OWN TIARA.

"A mutiny. Yeah, right." I laughed with him. "Why would we want to do that? Façade is so magical and . . . hey." I paused, like the thought had just occurred to me, but inside my heart was racing. "Speaking of, have you ever wondered where they get their magic?"

"From the earth," Reed said matter-of-factly. "That's part of what my parents do—they identify magical organisms, but also store some of their magic for Façade."

"They steal it?" I asked. What was Façade doing sucking power out of people when they had the whole earth?

"No, they just take a bit. The process doesn't affect the organism—it's like taking sap from a tree or wool from a sheep. Nature's MP isn't as strong as human MP, but there's plenty out there. And more than anything, Façade recognizes the importance of keeping that resource healthy."

Okay, what? Façade had an alternative power source, and they were still taking magic from unknowing humans, and using that magic ONLY on royals? Think of what they could do if they let those sub hopefuls keep their magic and use it to help everyday people instead.

"You'll learn about all of this during training, if you ever make it to Level Three," Reed said.

"I already did."

"Already what? Learned about magic?"

"No, I made Level Three. I mean, I don't know who I'll Match for or anything yet. I just found out I was moving up last week. Right before the play."

Reed looked confused. "But you said you just started working for the agency this summer."

"Yeah."

"People sub for years and years before they're able to

Match. Some people never even move up to Level Two." Reed shook his head. "So how did you . . . but that's impossible."

"Unlikely, but not impossible." I shrugged. "I guess I just got lucky."

Lucky, or the advancement was a bribe. Genevieve could have just erased my memory when I found out about the stolen magic, but my empathy was a very useful commodity for Façade. They wanted to keep me happy. Still, I was sure that they wouldn't hesitate to sanitize me if I went too far.

And I was planning on going too far.

"So you haven't had Level Three training yet?" he asked.

"Not exactly." I glanced up at the clock. Meredith would be here any minute. What if she was close enough to hear, or could override Reed's manual trick, or . . . read lips! If she knew, or anyone at Façade knew, what I was about to say, then my friendship with Reed *would* be forbidden. Telling him this put him in so much danger, I couldn't even pretend to know what might happen.

But I *needed* to tell him. Reed thought everything was wonderful. He'd spent his whole life training to be in this magical world. I had to tell him. HAD TO.

"Reed, listen—"

"Hey, I'm going to run to the bathroom before we have to leave—"

"No! Stop!" I stood up and grabbed him by the collar of his shirt so he was right in my face, so close I could count his eyelashes. He blinked at me, his smile amused but unsure. I sucked in a breath and let out the words I'd been holding in for too long. "You-should-know-that-Façade-also-takes-magic-from-subs-that-don't-make-it-past-the-trial-gig. They-don't-just-wash-their-memory-they-also-take-their-magic-and-store-it-and-use-the-magic-to-run-Façade-and . . . and . . ." I gulped in another breath. "Andthepeopleneverrememberthatithappened. They . . . have no choice."

I let go of his collar. The material was stretched where I'd pulled.

"No, I told you," Reed said. "My parents research this stuff for a living. Just last week we found a species of flower that has magical petals. And there's this tree, they've been researching it for years—"

"I'm sure that's all true, but so is this. And what they do to humans is not a sheep shearing. It's a violation."

I put my hands on my knees, still out of breath. Reed led me over to the table and crouched down so we were face to face. His eyes were closed, like he needed to shut down to digest what I'd just said. I closed my eyes too, still overwhelmed with the magic and adrenaline and excitement from finally sharing the truth.

"See?" said a voice from the doorway. "This is exactly what I was talking about. You start comparing experiences, and next thing you know, you're sitting by a tree, k-i-s-s-i-n-g."

I opened my eyes and let out a sigh. "Welcome back, Meredith."

Chapter
5

*M*eredith emerged from the shadows. Her outfit was classic Meredith—a sharp black business suit, her green hair in a tight bun. It had only been two weeks since I'd last seen her, but her petite frame looked even thinner, her eyes hollow despite the well-applied makeup.

"Another unexpected entrance," I said.

Reed hopped up. "Is this your agent?"

Meredith stretched out her hand. "Meredith Pouffinski, princess agent extraordinaire—"

"Or so she's been told," I finished.

"And you're Reed Pearson." Meredith gave Reed the once-over. "I worked with your mom for a bit, before she went over to Organic Magic. Lovely woman."

"Thank you. Nice to meet you." Reed wouldn't make eye contact with me. "I'm guessing Sergei will be here soon."

A dark blue bubble formed behind Reed, and out barged a middle-aged man. He wore jeans, a white T-shirt, motorcycle boots, and a leather jacket with an eagle on the front. He also sported a fabulous orange-and-red-streaked Mohawk. All the agents and counsel members at Façade colored their hair as a sort of status symbol, but I had a feeling Sergei would have colored his hair regardless.

"I am right here," Sergei boomed in a startling Russian accent. "And you should not delay. Royals are not of the patient type."

Reed slapped him on the back. "Serg, what's with the message? Are we in trouble? You haven't picked me up in your bubble since Level Two."

"I saw Meredith leaving the Façade, so I thought I would pick you up for your next position. For sake of old times." He winked at Meredith. "We do not have much opportunity to, how you say, *mingle* at work."

Meredith swallowed. I think she was trying not to throw up. Sergei was handsome enough, in his own gruff, biker way, but he wasn't Meredith's prince. "Yes, I'm very busy at work. Too busy for any extracurricular activity, I'm afraid."

"There is always time for fun." Sergei drew out the last word to hold significance. Meredith merely blinked.

Sergei shook his head. "But where are the manners? Reed, will you not introduce me to this girl?"

48

"I'm Desi," I said.

"Yes, I know." Sergei rubbed his nose. "You are a bit of celebrity to Façade now, Miss Bascomb. You have risen to great heights in very short time."

"Yes, she's a star," Meredith said. "I can't take all the credit for that. But I certainly take most." Meredith glanced down at her watch. "And now that we are all acquainted, we must rush to Façade. Perhaps we'll see you boys again?"

"That is my hope." Sergei punched Reed on the shoulder. "And I will scold my client about this date."

"Date?"

"It is not good to mix business with too much pleasure. A little mixing . . . That is all right."

Reed's face reddened. "We were just talking. You said it was allowed. Or is that forbidden now, too?"

"What is of more interest is why I could not hear your words when I turned on your surveillance," Sergei said.

I faked a frown. "Maybe it's broken? We were just talking about this stupid rumor that's going around the school. Oh, and the Winter Ball. I told Reed I'd help him set up some of the ice-skating stuff. If you guys get a chance, you should totally check out the sleigh rides—"

"I'll mark my calendar." Meredith yawned. "I'm sure whatever you two were talking about was far less important than what's happening right now at Façade."

I stole a glance at Reed. I couldn't get him to look at me.

"Sergei, it's been a, er . . . delight. As always," Meredith said.

"My delight, of course. Would be more delightful if you would let me take you on a date, yes?"

"Such a charmer." Meredith coughed. "And I do so love that jacket. Now, ta-ta!"

Sergei bowed before disappearing. Meredith pointed at me. "You have one minute. And no k-i-s-s-i—"

"I got it," I said.

She slipped inside her bubble.

"Wow, Sergei has himself a crush," I said. "That was so cute that he came here just to see more of Meredith—"

"Are you telling me the truth?" Reed cut me off. His voice came out broken. He still wasn't looking at me.

I nodded solemnly. "Yeah. It'd be better if I wasn't, but . . . yeah. All of it is true."

Without saying anything else, Reed stumbled into his bubble. I wish I could have figured out an easier way to talk to him about sub-sanitation. I wish we had more time to discuss it—maybe he would think of it as a necessary evil like Meredith and Genevieve did. Maybe I was just being dramatic.

Or maybe I was totally right, and Reed and I needed to get our own bubble and go save the subbing world *stat*.

"So, what are you doing here?" I asked, once I'd joined Meredith in the bubble.

Meredith took some hand lotion out of her desk and rubbed it into her fingers. "Every time I visit Dubai, my hands dry out. Granted, I adore Princess Alice and Princess Lucy, but the least they could do is offer some moisturizer."

"Mer? Hello?"

"You have work, of course. Now, sit." She motioned to the plush black leather chair in her front waiting area. "And for the millionth time, don't call me Mer." She got busy making herself a coffee and me a hot chocolate. She even plopped in marshmallows. I loved how well she knew me, loved our little bubble office briefings. And honestly, I loved this job. If I didn't know what I knew, I could sub forever with Meredith, and be perfectly happy.

But marshmallows or not, I did know, and there was no turning back.

"I am so slammed right now." Meredith downed her coffee in two quick gulps. "They're hosting a celebration today for my promotion, but since no one but Genevieve knows I've been promoted, my workload is still ridiculous."

"So, that promotion?" I set my mug down on her glass coffee table. "You really got it?"

A slow grin spread across her face. "Yes. It'll be official today. I'm the youngest council member at twenty-nine."

"You're twenty-nine?" Meredith was young, but not that young.

"Ish. Thirty-two. Thirty-five, tops. But still the youngest. It's the biggest thing that's ever happened to me, that's for sure." Meredith lifted up my mug and wiped away the condensation mark. I looked at her hands, so tiny and graceful and . . . ringless.

I don't know why this surprised me, but it did. Back when Meredith was a sub, she'd fallen in a love with a prince. As far as Façade's rules went, this one was The Grand Master Broken Rule. Another agent, Lilith—my Level One trainer and Meredith's enemy—spilled the beans on the secret relationship, and Meredith almost lost her job. She broke up with her prince, but they had recently gotten back together. Right after she'd gotten the big promotion, he'd sent her a text saying, MARRY ME. Hey, not the most romantic proposal, but it's not like he could drop by in a hot-air balloon when they had to keep it all hush-hush. I didn't know how Meredith answered him—if she was secretly engaged now, or if they'd broken up because of the promotion.

"So, speaking of biggest things that ever happened to you, any other news?" I asked.

Meredith narrowed her eyes. "You know about my promotion. Pay increase of thirty percent."

"Right, but is your status in any other area changing? Like, relationships?" I pointed discreetly at her finger. She slipped her hand into her suit pocket.

"My credit card company just upgraded me to platinum," she said icily. "That's about it."

So that would either be a *no* or an *I'm not telling you*. And the snippiness was undoubtedly because she knew what my opinion would be on the matter—take the prince, drop Façade. But for Meredith, her job came before everything, even a proposal from a prince.

"We're almost at Façade. You might as well read about

your assignment. I just have to check on something at the agency, and then we'll get you going." Meredith slipped into her office, probably to get away from my questions. I still didn't know what "work" was ahead of me.

I thumbed through my manual. The princess's profile was up already. I'd spent months preparing for my first Level Two job, which ended up being one night at an art gallery. And now, here I was at Level Three, with "Build up tolerance to pain" promising who-knows-what horrors, and I had only watched some TV and plucked some nose hairs. I wasn't ready for this.

I really wasn't.

PRINCESS VANNA

Age: 16

Hometown: Kamigano in the Far East

Favorite Color: Black

Favorite Book: *The Bourne Identity*

Favorite Food: Food is fuel

Family Background: My father is the crown prince of Kamigano. This means he is next to rule, after my grandparents, the emperor and empress. After him? My baby brother, Kaito, who turns one next month. Yes, in Kamigano, the youngest male heir still rules over the oldest girl. I don't fault the baby for that. What I *do* hate is how my parents, not to mention the entire country, are so enraptured by this baby cooing or spitting up peas on the latest news segment that *actual* news is going unnoticed.

Attention, viewers! Sorry to interrupt coverage on a recent natural disaster. We'll get to that in the second half of the news program. Right now—the Prince of Peas!

Truly, it's not like we *rule* anything. I would like to feel like I could make more of a difference, and I'm not talking about giving hugs to schoolchildren at media events. I want to be more than the face of the government, I want to be *part* of the government. That's why I'm leaving. To prove I can be more by doing more. I know my parents have different expectations, but I need to break out.

Cultural Traditions: Our family is revered by our people. There are special prayers said daily for the royal family. Because we are such a vital representation of this country, my father wants me to be as regal and groomed as possible. He encourages my talents in sculpture, gymnastics, fencing, and I dabble a bit in the martial arts. Janin, my assistant, will tell you where you need to be and when. She's a bit of a bore, but she gets the job done. My maid, Sora, also helps with some . . . special skills on the side. Purely for recreation.

My family and I are kept very well guarded at the castle, but you will, of course, be expected to attend meetings and events. During my absence, I've ensured that my schedule is light.

Anything Else We Should Know: You're a stand-in, so please don't offer opinions. I've had subs in the past act strange, and my family was suspicious. I usually keep to myself, except with Sora, and my parents really don't notice me much lately, so I doubt they'd pick up on odd behavior. But do make sure every member of my family and everyone on the staff sees you regularly. Sees you, but doesn't hear you. Always keep track of where you have been and where you are. Don't trust anyone outside of family and Sora—in fact, sleep with one eye open. Stay on your toes. And, of course, stay alive.

Um.

Uh.

Er.

So.

Okay? *Stay alive?* I had a feeling watching a million kung fu movies was not going to prepare me for this gig.

I had an awful thought. Was Façade trying to get rid of me? Because, sorry, most princesses talked about bullies or crushes. They didn't foreshadow *mortal danger*.

I pounded on Meredith's wall. Her door flew open. "You look green."

"You're one to talk."

"Why, thank you. I had a dye touch-up before the meeting." Meredith patted her chartreuse hair. "Why are you pounding? What's wrong? Are you ill?"

"What, no. I'm fabulous." I jabbed Meredith with my manual. "I just love profiles that tell me to sleep with one eye open. Cozies me up like a nice security blanket."

"You're worried?" she asked, although her voice really said, *I can't believe you're worried or complaining*. Which,

55

actually, is always what her voice sounded like. "You have nothing to worry about. She's just being funny."

"About death."

"Death. Please. Genevieve obviously doesn't think you need any more preparation. This job will be your chance to prove your worth, ensuring you're Matched to a very desirable royal."

"Wow. I feel much better about the whole I'm-going-to-die thing." I gave Meredith an exaggerated thumbs-up. "Why don't you drop me off right now?"

"About that." Meredith braced herself against the doorway as her bubble landed. I pitched forward, but caught myself on her arm.

"We're here," I said.

"Maybe not the here you think. We're at Façade. You're not going to your next job in my bubble. You're going in yours."

"But I don't have a bubble."

She closed her eyes and shook her head. "Your deductive reasoning really astounds me."

"You mean . . . I get my own bubble?"

Meredith led me out of the entryway and into the Façade lobby. "Yes. Welcome to Level Three."

Chapter
6

Meredith glanced down at her manual. "I have a quick errand to run. Why don't you wait here in the lobby and I'll pick up your bubble on my way back. You still have a half hour until you need to be on your job."

"Yeah, okay. I'll be here." I considered wandering back to the sub-sanitation room, but that field trip might have been a one-shot trip, and I needed more of a plan first. Maybe I could learn something useful from the royal relics littering the lobby. At least take some time to strategize for my next assignment. Or run away from it.

The grandeur and sheer size of the room still astounded me, largely because Façade was housed inside the Tour

Montparnasse in Paris, one of the few modern skyscrapers in the city. From the outside, you would have no clue that something like Façade could fit in here—and for good reason. Façade was far bigger than the "floor" it took up in the building. The explanation was the same they used for nearly everything: magic!

There wasn't a museum in the world that had a more extensive collection of royal memorabilia. Swords from long-lost battles, thrones from fallen empires. And my favorite—the tiara wall. Yeah, sorry. I still wanted a tiara.

I would research the other items in a minute. I had a mission, after all. But for now, the shiny sparkles and jewels called to me. I pushed my face against the glass.

"Miss Bascomb?"

I didn't move. "Yeah?"

"May I help you with something? Would you like to try one on?"

I suctioned myself off and spun around. Ferdinand, the receptionist, sat at the front desk, smiling kindly. I'd never really spoken to him, just some quick pleasantries whenever I zipped in and out of Façade. "Seriously? We can do that?"

He jingled a set of keys. "For a Level Three? Certainly."

I put on Princess Grace's first. Of course I did. Grace Kelly was one of my favorite actresses, who later married the Prince of Monaco. And to wear something *she* wore? Forget about it. The tiara was surprisingly light and thin. The comb caught in my hair when I took it off, and Ferdinand had to untwist it for me.

"Thanks," I said. "I can't believe they let us wear the tiaras. What if someone tries to take one?"

"Façade has installed a tracking device on all the royal artifacts in this room. In fact, they have secretly installed the same device on most major royal heirlooms—crown jewels, priceless art, thrones, ancient weaponry. It's all itemized in our system—you can log on right now and see where Princess Kate's sapphire ring is, and by extension Princess Kate, since she's probably wearing it." He winked. "It's a fun application to fiddle with when things are slow here. The royals have no clue how much we know."

"But aren't you worried about a sub stealing something?"

"That's part of why we do the trace. Invented the program after a notorious former employee turned into a jewel thief."

"Yeah, I've heard about her," I grumbled, annoyed that the one bad seed was always used as an example of what could go wrong.

"Do you want to try on any others?" Ferdinand asked.

"No. I'm good." I gazed up at the tiaras. Part of me wanted to try on every one of them, but I needed to use my alone time to get some answers. Maybe Ferdinand would know something about the sub-sanitation room. "Hey, Ferdinand, how long have you worked at Façade?"

"Sixty-five years."

"For real? How old are you? Wait, sorry, that's rude. Don't answer that. I mean, unless you want—"

"I am eighty-two. I began working for Façade at seventeen."

"So, did you sub?"

"For a short amount of time, yes."

"Oh. And then . . ."

"And then I moved around departments until I finally settled at the front desk. I've been happy here—I have the opportunity to meet many employees on their very first day."

"So you've, like, seen everything, huh?" I asked.

Ferdinand set Princess Grace's crown back on the purple velvet pillow. "Not everything. Just the beginnings of everything."

It's funny, because here I was scrambling around trying to think of an ally, when I already knew, or at least kind of knew, someone at Façade who knew *everyone*. "Ferdinand, did I mention how nice you look today?"

"No. But I look very much the same every day, Miss Bascomb." Ferdinand locked the door to the tiara case and hobbled back to his desk. He was so venerable and ancient, as much a part of Façade's history as the relics surrounding him. "I'm not a dinner roll," he said, once he was back behind his desk and had a chance to catch his breath, "so care to tell me why you are buttering me up?"

I leaned on the high counter. "I just never get a chance to talk to someone who has worked here so long. You must have crazy stories."

"I'm also excellent at staying quiet."

"Stories are meant to be shared. Unless they're *secret* stories?"

"Again, quiet."

"Okay, but there has to be one story that is too good to keep to yourself. Something that's been *boiling* in you forever."

Ferdinand shook his head.

"Really?" I asked. "Nothing? Not even gossip. Or maybe some little-known background or history or . . . something no one else knows?"

"I can give you a tour of the displays. But something tells me that's not what you're asking."

"Not really."

"It's refreshing to chat, since most subs just bounce by my desk. However, I do have other duties. So I hope you'll afford me enough respect to tell me what exactly it is you want?"

What did I want? I could write a list longer than the copy of the Magna Carta they had over in the case. Oh. Unless that *was* the Magna Carta.

"I don't know, Ferdinand. There is just so much to figure out here, it's like the more I learn, the more I realize I don't know anything at all."

"That's called wisdom."

"Yeah, well, then wisdom stinks." When I first started working here, this place was still amazing and perfect. Subbing was the dream job I didn't even know existed. Now, only a few months had passed, and already I had a whole different point of view. I wondered what kind of shifts Ferdinand had witnessed in his sixty-plus years here. "Right. So I do have a question. This place, it's magical, right? And the job—the best. But if you could change anything about the agency, what would it be and why?"

Ferdinand drummed his fingers on his desk. "No one has ever asked me that. Usually, the only question I get is which way to the bathroom."

"Look at all the wisdom those people are missing."

"More buttering, hmmm?" He scratched his chin. "Very well. I'll play along. You know what I've always wondered? Why isn't there a division that specializes in global diplomacy, international peace treaties, war negotiations? We have access to more than half of the countries in this world, and we have never brought them together. There might be some secret sector I know nothing about. But all that money put into makeup?" Ferdinand shrugged. "Makeup isn't life altering. I would wager to guess Façade could create world peace if they tried."

I nearly leaned over the desk and kissed Ferdinand on the cheek. Finally, someone who understood! "Exactly! Ferdinand, think of how much *possibility* is in this room."

"Not possibility, just the past—battles, forgotten kingdoms, greed. All by-products of power." Ferdinand clicked onto his computer and read through something on the screen. "Here's one bit of advice. At a place like this, don't be a chief. It's best to stay out of the way, keep your head down, and do your job."

"But—"

He glanced up at me, his eyes twinkling. "That way no one suspects it's you when something happens."

I widened my eyes. Did Ferdinand have any idea what I really was asking? Did I even know what I asking, what I hoped to accomplish? "Oh. Yeah. Okay."

"And now, Miss Bascomb, I've quite enjoyed our talk, but I must return to my duties and you to yours. Best of luck subbing for Princess Vanna."

"Princess Vanna? How do you know who I'm subbing for?" I asked.

He peered up at me. "Because I *do*."

Could I adopt him? Is that possible? Hide Ferdinand in the guest bedroom and feed him peanut butter sandwiches while we devise a grand scheme to equalize Façade? Is there a non-psycho way to ask him that?

I didn't have time to find out, because Meredith bustled into the lobby. "Ready?"

"Sure. Thanks, Ferdinand. Keep it real."

"I shall try."

Ferdinand confirmed that not everyone here was drinking the crazy punch. Some people saw flaws, and maybe he was also trying to make changes, in his own quiet way. Maybe change wasn't as impossible as I'd thought.

Meredith wordlessly pointed her remote at a space between the reception desk and the sitting area. Ferdinand didn't even blink when a sunny yellow bubble dripped into the air. I involuntarily took a step toward the cute little orb of wonder—I couldn't explain how, but I knew this belonged to me.

"Go on. Take a look," Meredith said.

I'd been inside Meredith's luxurious office/bubble and two rickety emergency bubbles. This was somewhere in between. Although not fancy, there was a calm cheerfulness about the space, inspired mostly by the funky daisy rug. Pushed under the control panel was a red faux-fur-lined swivel chair, and on the wall was a movie poster of Audrey Hepburn, the one from *Breakfast at Tiffany's*. It's like someone jumped into my brain, took notes, and then Desied the place up.

"I am in love." I placed my hand over my heart. I had my own bubble. I still wouldn't be able to drive a car for over a year. But I could go anywhere in the world in this thing. I sat down in the chair and twirled. "I have my own bubbblllllle!!!"

Meredith grabbed the sides of the chair and looked me in the eye. "This is a company bubble. You don't own it. You're only allowed to use it for work purposes."

"What if I need to research castles? Can I go to Buckingham Palace?"

Meredith shrugged. "Sure. If you get your homework done first."

"I'll have the queen help me with my algebra." I ran my hands over the panel screen. The words DESTINATION: KAMIGANO was already inputted. Just type in a location and I could go there. This was magical.

Oh. This was *magical*.

I drew my hands away like they'd been burned. "How does this bubble move?"

"It's obviously our economy-size model, so not as quickly as mine, but far smoother than an emergency clunker—"

"No, I mean . . ." I lowered my voice. "Is this bubble run by magic?"

"No, we have an antigravitational chamber in here. Of course it's magic."

"Stolen?"

"How would I know? Magic is accessed from many sources, you know. This one might be juiced by a cuddly kitten."

"If they can just use kittens, then why mess with people—"

"Façade does not *mess* with people. And people happen to be a hundred times more magical than anything else. So stop asking about that. It's a brick wall, darling."

I ran my hand along the adorable chair. Okay, so I had to use the bubble to get to this job. And this job was somehow going to teach me more about subbing or myself or this agency. And once I learned . . . whatever it was I was going to learn, then I could go back to Façade and . . . uh . . . better mankind. So using this bubble now was just a means to an end. I'd make up for it later. Besides, the fur on the chair was really soft.

Meredith leaned down and air-kissed my cheeks. "Make sure you put on your rouge. When you're done, type in *home* and the bubble will know where to go. Hit the bubble

65

button on your manual and it will suck back in. I'll be in touch with information about your Match when we have it. Now, I have to get back for my first meeting on the council. Are you ready for this job?"

Even the beauty of the bubble couldn't erase the horror of the BEST requirements or the fear of my impending gig. Could I fake a stomachache? Send another girl while I hung out in my bubble, maybe twirl around in the chair more? "This place I'm going now. Meredith, am I really going to be okay?"

"You have your manual for emergencies. You have your bubble for catastrophes. And, Desi, you have your magic."

I didn't feel completely assured, but I opted to go through with it, my drive to figure out the inner workings of Façade stronger than my fear. The bubble rose the moment Meredith stepped out, tilting me back in my seat. It was true, the ride wasn't as seamless as Meredith's, but not nearly as jarring as emergency bubbles. There was a constant, airplanelike hum.

I used my time to master stealth. Which means I tried to catch the fly that had somehow buzzed into my vehicle. But then it accidentally flew through the permeable part of the bubble wall. I hoped he liked his new home over Russia, or wherever we were.

"Please ensure that you are properly fastened," said a chipper electronic voice. "We're beginning our initial descent." Five minutes later, the bubble sank to the ground. "Thank you for flying with me, Desi. I look forward to transporting you upon completion of your job."

"Thanks?" I said out loud. Was I supposed to talk back to my bubble? Should I name her. I was thinking Daisy. She looked like a Daisy.

"Please exit, Desi."

"Okay, Daisy."

"I thought your name is Desi."

Hey! She really was talking directly to me; she wasn't just programmed. "I am Desi. But I just decided that you should be called Daisy. Daisy, the bubble."

The bubble didn't answer. She was probably too over-joyed to speak.

"Well, ta-ta, darling!" I made a grand bow before taking a step backward, hoping I'd at least have a chance to get my bearings before the royal ninjas attacked.

Chapter 7

The view in front of me was so acutely beautiful, it felt like I was in a perfectly staged movie scene. The royal fountain was like something out of *The King and I*, with blazing red trees dripping leaves into the water. Koi fish glittered under the surface, and crickets chirped behind me. Lacy gray flowers kissed the cool air with sage. Through a break in the grove, I could just make out the castle, but not the kind you see at Disneyland. The architectural Asian wonder had a jade-green roof sloping upward on each of the castle's many, many tiers. I hoped Vanna's vacation was a long one. I could use a little tranquility.

Well, as tranquil as I could be, with instructions like "stay alive" on the profile.

I sat on a stone bench in the palace gardens while I waited for the Royal Rouge to literally work its magic. One quick swipe from my gold compact resulted in a transformation about fifteen minutes later, and it was always fascinating taking on the new princess's identity.

Vanna's arms and calves were fiercely sculpted. I was always me when I took on these forms—meaning I had my own mind, own clumsiness, own free will—but I couldn't help but feel tougher in this athletic build. I wanted to drop and do fifty push-ups, just to prove I could, although it would not be very ladylike in the stiff pencil skirt and silk suit jacket Vanna wore. Not the everyday wardrobe of a sixteen-year-old.

Someone called Vanna's name. I wasn't sure if I should respond or run, if the caller was Vanna's friend or foe. Surely she had bodyguards, right? I cleared my throat and let out a feeble "Here?"

Moments later, a woman burst into the peaceful courtyard. Her graying hair flew out of her bun. She wore a tailored suit similar to mine. "Princess Vanna!" She bowed. She did not look at me as she spoke. "You must stop doing this to us. We are simply trying to do our job, which is protecting you."

"Protecting me from what?" I asked.

She pulled out a walkie-talkie. "This is Janin. The tiger has been spotted. I repeat, the tiger is spotted. Over."

My heart skipped a beat for a second, until I realized that

I must be the tiger. Hey, you never know what kind of pets these royals keep.

"Princess Vanna, there is no room in your schedule for disappearing acts. I know that meet and greet was insufferable, but you can't just flee to the gardens."

"Sorry, Janin," I said.

"You have approximately fifteen minutes to change into your training clothing and meet your instructor in the gymnasium. And be forewarned—she's very determined for you to land that back-handspring combination before the documentary film crew comes this evening."

I'd found that the best way to learn what was on the princess's schedule was to pretend that she forgot. The technique usually led to exasperation, but at least I got answers. "Film crew. Um, that's tonight?"

"You know it's tonight! This is the first time cameras have had access inside the palace, the first time the crown jewels have been on full display, the first time our royalty has exposed their daily life."

"You mean, their human side," I said. I'd picked up on this theme in my manual research. In many cultures, royals are still considered to be almost godlike—certainly not like everyday people with everyday problems who just happen to be born into an extraordinary situation.

Janin pretended she didn't hear me. "Your younger brother may take that first step, and of course the country will want to see that!"

"Wait. Rewind. So I have to do a back handspring and

the baby just has to walk?" I tried to keep the panic from edging into my voice.

"Please, Your Highness. Your time is limited."

"But, seriously. I'm good at so many other things. Lock picking! Here, give me a bobby pin and about an hour, and I can maybe unlock something."

"You chose to do gymnastics yourself. The film crew has already blocked out the space. There is no changing your activity now."

She led me away from the fountain, across an arched bridge over a lily-covered pond. As I stumbled ahead in Vanna's practical-but-not-for-ancient-stone heels, I scrambled to come up with a plan, because how things looked now . . . I was in royal doo-doo.

A back handspring. I couldn't even do a cartwheel. The second I got into that gymnasium, the instructor would figure me out. And then . . . a film crew? What if they wanted me to do karate, too? Why hadn't they given me more time to prepare? It would be physically impossible to get out of Vanna's tight schedule today.

I stopped walking. Wait. Unless I *made it* physically possible.

An injury would mean Vanna would be laid up, then *I* would be laid up, which would save me from being caught, or sub spotted, if I failed to do a simple somersault. A sub spotting would mean the end of my job, the end of my magical research. My magic would be just another vial on Ye Ol' Wall of MP.

I surveyed the landscape. Back near the fountain, the trees were dense—I could run into something there, but we were too far now. The inner gardens were just a few yards away, and once I reached those, the pathway would be smooth and obstacle-free. My only chance of making something happen was here on the old bridge. Maybe the pond . . . No, I couldn't just flop into a pond. What if it wasn't deep enough?

I would have to trip. Really trip, *face-plant* trip, so I would definitely get hurt. Unlike athletic feats, tripping was something I could do. Unfortunately, I would be the one hurt, not Vanna. Even after the rouge wore off and I was back to Desi, that injury would stay.

I *knew* this gig was going to cause me physical harm. But there wasn't any other option. I would lose much more then my dignity and health if that film crew documented my attempt at gymnastics. I had just a few more steps on the bridge. I had to do a fall. Now.

I faked an unconvincing stumble, but when I did, my heel really *did* catch on a stone, sending my weight sideways. My knee slammed into the low stone wall before I catapulted over the bridge and into the lily pond, which, it turned out, was shallow enough that the pond floor knocked the wind out of me. I pushed some sludge out of my eyes and looked up at an ashen-faced Janin. My knee and ankle were already throbbing.

Mission . . . accomplished. I guess.

* * *

A flurry of nurses hoisted me onto a stretcher and into the palace. My tour of the beautiful building was minimal, since all I saw was ceiling. I was brought into Vanna's lavender-and-gray room, where attendants helped bathe me and dress me in a silk kimono, before a doctor analyzed my injuries. I had a large contusion on my knee and a small ankle sprain. As far as intentional wounds go, I'd done pretty well—I'd be laid up at least until next week, and I would probably be gone before that. I was propped up onto pillows, given almond cookies and green tea, and left to rest.

Why hadn't I thought of injuring myself before? When I was Floressa Chase, I had to roller skate around a yacht—one slip could have bought me days of R & R. And if I stocked up on some fake blood, every sub job would be a breeze.

There was a quick rap on the door.

"Uh, you may enter!" I called.

A young woman, maybe in her early twenties, hurried in, wheeling a cart filled with all sorts of cleaning supplies. Even in her frumpy maid uniform, she was ethereal—lean frame, glowing skin, and brown almond-shaped eyes. So this was Vanna's friend Sora. I thought maid meant something like maiden or lady-in-waiting, but nope. Maid meant maid.

"You alone?" she asked.

I nodded.

She grabbed my knee and squeezed.

I yowled in pain. Who did this girl think she was?

She flopped down next to me on the bed. "Just making sure you weren't faking."

"No, I'm not faking. That really hurt!"

"I can't believe you hurt your knee. This will put your training back *weeks*."

I leaned back on the pillow, the pain still hot in my leg. "It was an accident."

"Rule number four fifty-three. Accidents can kill."

I tried to keep the annoyance off my face. No duh, accidents kill. What was rule number four thirty-two? Brush your teeth?

Her expression turned thoughtful. "Since your stunt training is canceled, we'll have to shift our focus to mental strengthening exercises. And security systems. You've been falling behind there. And for how much you're paying me, I want you to be fully prepared." She stood, and in one fluid motion, ripped off her dress. The garment fell to the floor. Underneath, Sora had on a black Lycra catsuit, complete with zippers and mini computer doohickeys and wires. She looked like she was about to rob an art museum. She kicked the dress into a corner. "Of all my covers, this maid job has been the worst. I really wish you'd let me go for gardener instead. I like those sun hats."

I didn't answer, just stared at Sora in her sleek outfit. Security systems? Her cover. Was Sora . . . Was she a spy? If she was, what did that make Vanna?

Sora reached into her cart and pulled out a thin silver laptop. Within seconds, she'd plugged cords from inside the mop into the computer and converted the Windex bottle into a camera, creating a complex technological hub. "No offense, Van, but you tripped on a bridge? How are you going to qualify for the most elite covert government organization in all of Asia when you can't even walk around your own palace?"

"I said—"

"It was an accident. Yeah, yeah."

Sora busied herself with her spy gear. I wasn't as dumb as I looked. In the last hour, I'd avoided a sub spotting, blown Sora's cover, and figured out why Vanna left. She wanted to work for the government, but not as a princess. And all her extracurriculars doubled as prep for her dream job.

Despite the pain, I couldn't help but be giddy. Forget karate princess. Spy princess was going to be perfect Façade prep.

"So." I smiled at Sora. "Learning to crack security systems sounds like a *perfect* lesson for today."

Chapter
8

Sora was worth every penny Vanna was paying her, because not only did we cover security systems, but also how to pick locks (seriously, I was getting good at this one), how to turn a cell phone into a mobile bug, how to dodge alarm lasers, and how to watch facial cues for signs of deceit. And she managed to wax the floor and dust the furniture, all within a few hours.

"Now I want to see you use some of the lesson on manipulation we had last week." Sora helped me hop back into bed. Janin would be in soon to wake me up from my "nap." "Good spies don't show authentic emotion, unless it's part of their cover. The part you need to work on playing is that of a contented daughter, not a princess jealous of her little brother."

"Who says I'm jealous?" I asked.

"You do, every time you look at him or your parents. It's spelled out on your face. And your parents are worried, and if they worry, they'll focus more attention on you, and the last thing a spy needs—"

"Is attention," I finished. Of course. This is the same thing Ferdinand said—stay off the radar; don't make yourself a suspect. "So I will play the part of the happy injured princess."

"But not injured too long. We only have two weeks to complete your application project, although I'm starting to wonder if you should wait a year."

I didn't know what this application project was, but my guess was it had something to do with the government agency Vanna wanted to work for. Of course, I couldn't ask, especially someone as sharp as Sora, so I just nodded. Besides, I'd probably be gone in two weeks, and Vanna would be miraculously recovered as soon as she got back.

Sora threw her maid costume on and grabbed her feather duster. "I can smell Janin's perfume. She's around the corner, down the hall, advancing . . ." Sora sniffed again. "Six-point-three seconds away. I'm gone. Remember your cover!" Sora gave me a jaunty little bow and scuttled out of the room. I lay back on my pillows and closed my eyes. Janin knocked softly on the door.

"Your Highness? It's time." She pushed a wheelchair

into the room, and I pretended to wake up. "His Majesty, your father, understands that gymnastics are impossible, so they've changed your schedule."

I let her help me into the wheelchair. "Good. So we just have to watch my brother be a baby."

"Well, yes, that, but His Majesty didn't want to pass up the opportunity to showcase your talents, and the purpose of this documentary is to highlight the skills of the royal family, after all." She pushed me into the hallway, where three more women waited to help escort me to the dining hall. "Escorting" involved them shuffling behind us, heads bowed. It amazed me all the stupid jobs royalty created.

"But I'm practically immobile," I said.

"Which is why they're setting up in the studio."

"Studio?" Spy or no spy, I could not help the worry that crept into my voice.

"Of course. Your art is of great interest to your people. I'm sure they'd love to see what you create using raw clay."

I leaned back in my wheelchair and sighed. Tumbling out and breaking my wrist probably wasn't an option. Which meant I'd have to rely on my next asset if I was going to display Vanna's "talent" for sculpture to her whole country.

Magic time.

While the camera crew set up, another team got to work fixing my hair and applying my makeup. I was changed into a high-necked floral blouse paired with slim jeans. A burly man in the camera crew scooped me up and arranged me on a sculptor's stool, in front of a slab of muddy clay. The studio had finished pieces lined up against the wall. Vanna's work consisted of birds of prey—sharp angles, fierce poses, all lifelike. These were museum-worthy, not something I could whip up on the spot. Not something I could whip up with years of training.

The director bowed at me from behind the camera. "So this first shot will be basic. I want to get a glimpse of your creative process. Then we'll show some art you've already done, add some music and voice-over as you work. We'll save interview questions for later."

"So I just need to make something with this clay," I said.

"Yes, Your Highness. Pretend we aren't even here. Let your creativity guide you."

I stared at the clay and bit my lip. T-shirts. T-shirts were my artistic medium. The best I could make out of this clay was a ball, maybe a snowman if I got really inspired.

I stuck my fingers into the clay. A cameraman stepped closer in anticipation. I shot a look at Janin, who mouthed, "Create."

Create. Gah. Sub spotting here I come.

I unstuck a piece of clay and rolled it into a tube, like I used to do with my Play-Doh. When I was, oh, five. I stared at the tube, hoping it would transform into something resembling art. Maybe a scary snake?

I was saved by a quick rustling. Everyone dropped to the ground in a flurry of low bows. I glanced up to see the crown prince—a somber man with a penetrating gaze that probably inspired Vanna's sculptures. He gave my shoulder a quick but firm squeeze.

"Daughter, I came as soon as I was able. I'm so sorry about your injury." His forehead wrinkled in concern as he looked down at my ankle. "It's not like you to stumble, given your athletic training."

"I know," I said. "Bad luck."

"I'm sure you'll be equally impressive displaying your art."

"I'll try."

"I know how you feel about the press, but"—he lowered his voice—"this documentary is important for our family, and thus, important for the country, important to me—" He looked past me and his eyes lit up. "Aha! There's my little prince. Come, come. It's been ages since I've seen my boy."

His wife, the crown princess, laughed as she entered the room and handed her son to his father. They didn't seem aware of anyone else in the room or of the cameras turned to capture this moment.

I sat there on my stool, poking the clay. The wave of empathy, of magic, was instant and natural. Oh, Vanna. Perfect little brother, perfect family, and here she was trying to prove that she was something—someone—besides a princess. I knew that feeling so well, that twisted mix of love and jealousy and confusion. I'd lived that when Gracie was born. Not to mention, I knew what it was like to be different— I had a beauty queen mother who loved me, but often didn't understand me. Which is different than wanting to be a spy instead of a royal, but the emotions were the same.

The tingling worked down into my fingers as I molded the clay. I closed my eyes, not listening to anyone else, just tuning into the intensity of the moment. I don't know how much time passed, but when I opened my eyes, I had the beginnings of a bird. A crane, actually, with impossibly skinny legs and a graceful neck. It didn't have the same sharp angles as Vanna's work, but this was just a start, and . . . it worked. This was better than anything I could have created on my own. My magic worked to help a princess. I did exactly what I'd wanted to do.

"Perfect, Your Highness!" the director called out. "We'll speed up the frames, add some music, have you talk about your work . . . Just perfect. Even better than the gymnastics bit would have been."

I didn't even notice that the crown prince was standing right behind me. He looked down at me with pride. "Everything my daughter touches turns to gold. She's a magical girl."

You have no idea.

The camera crew began to pack up, and Janin stepped in to wheel me over to the sink to wash my hands.

Prince Kaito started to kick in his mother's arms. "No, Kaito. This studio is dirty."

He squirmed some more, and she finally sighed and set him down. He popped right up into a standing position.

"Oh, he's going to do it," Janin whispered. "This couldn't be any more perfect."

Kaito flashed a smile at the crew, already fumbling for the cameras. It was like he knew to wait, knew what his duty was. The crown prince held out his arms in delight. Kaito lifted a chubby thigh and took one step. We beamed, not wanting to cheer just yet, but all aware how big this moment was. The whole country would get to witness his first step.

But before the prince could walk any more, an alarm blared. We covered our ears. Kaito flopped onto the ground and started to bawl. His mother scooped him up.

A guard rushed in. "The crown jewels! Your Majesty, someone has stolen the crown jewels!"

And then the smoke bomb went off.

Chapter
9

The room erupted into chaos. Men in black suits spilled into the studio, circling around each royal and rushing us out. Janin kept her hands firmly on my wheelchair, insisting that she push me through the smoke-filled hallways. We coughed our way through corridor after corridor, following the set escape route. The grand front hall was a mass of people—military, police, paramedics, and more men in black suits. So many people crowded in to "help" that the end result was disorder.

Janin leaned down and whispered, "I know an easier way out to the garden that'll be safer."

She took a quick right down another hall and then

another, until I could hardly hear the sirens. At first, I was grateful just to be away from the crowd—my leg had been bumped twice already. But after the fourth turn, I was starting to get worried. "This doesn't look like there's an exit," I said. "Maybe we should go back."

"Don't worry, Desi, Your job is just about done."

I turned around in the chair as much as I could. Desi? HOW DID JANIN KNOW MY NAME? "What are you talking . . . Who are you?"

Janin stopped at a door and knocked four times. She wheeled me into the darkened space. I tried to stand up, but she pushed me back down in my seat.

"Took you long enough," said a voice that was obviously trying to sound deeper than it was. A flashlight went on, right in my face, so I couldn't see who was shining it. What I did see, though, was the shiner's pants. Black, tight. A catsuit just like the one Sora had on earlier.

Traitor.

"Did she put the makeup on yet?"

"Didn't have time," Janin said. "We're lucky I got her away from security."

"I think she'll change on her own now that I'm here," the voice said again.

"Did you get the jewels?" Janin asked.

"They're in my backpack."

"Sora!" I shouted. "This is illegal! I command you to, uh, unhand me. Take me back to my parents before they arrest you."

There was laughter. Eerily familiar laughter. The lights flicked on to reveal a messy office, perhaps belonging to someone on the staff. There was a futon to my right and a mini-fridge. Sitting on the desk was a girl in a catsuit, and she looked nothing like Sora.

The girl looked like Vanna. Sort of. She was a little taller, her nose a little pointier, her hair shorter . . . It's like someone took each of Vanna's features and smudged them with a rubber eraser.

The girl smiled. "Sorry to drop in like this, but when you twisted your ankle, it kind of put a damper on things."

"Who are you?"

"Vanna."

"No," I said. "*I'm* Vanna."

"No, Desi." She let out a patient sigh. "You're my sub."

"How did you . . . What's going on here?" Maybe this was Vanna's cousin, or a body double. When royals left their real life for the Façade Resort, they took on the identity of old celebrities so they wouldn't be recognized. Vanna should look like some dead actress, not an altered version of herself. "Vanna is supposed to be vacationing on a remote island."

"I'm going to go release another smoke bomb in the hallway," Janin said. "In case we were followed."

"Good idea." Vanna, or whoever this girl was, beamed at me as Janin stepped out of the room. "Why are you still looking at me like that?"

"If you don't tell me what's going on, I'll run . . . I'll wheel out there and find security."

"I needed a decoy. When I told your agency that I didn't want to use their celebrity makeup line, they offered a new product. Image shifting. The makeup altered my appearance enough that I could still pull off this . . . Well, it's kind of an audition for a new job."

"So you've been here the whole time? Why didn't you tell me what was going on?"

"I couldn't risk you telling anyone—" The lights shut off again. Someone knocked Vanna to the floor. I wheeled my chair back and was just able to reach the light switch. Now there were *two* girls in catsuits on the ground.

"Sora, it's me!" Vanna cried. "It's Vanna."

"That's Vanna!" Sora pointed at me, but when she looked at me, her expression hardened. I must have transformed back to Desi already. "Wait, who are you? What did you do with the princess?"

I usually had a few minutes once the princess returned before the rouge wore off and I was back to looking like me. Those few minutes were up. Vanna stood, finally looking like herself. "That's my sub. I needed her to finish my assignment."

"What's a sub? Where did you find a look-alike?" Sora stared at me with suspicion. "What is going on here? Your assignment isn't for another two weeks. And why are you standing on your injured ankle?"

"This girl is my decoy," Vanna said. "I knew you would say I wasn't ready to take on an assignment."

Sora knocked on Vanna's forehead. "Hello? You *weren't*

86

ready. We still have to go through infiltration, interrogation, hypnosis, and advanced weaponry."

"Sora, I'm golden. I stole the jewels. Look, they're in my pack." Vanna disappeared under the desk. She frowned when she hoisted up the bag. "Wait." She rummaged inside and looked up with wide eyes. "The jewels were in my backpack."

Sora pointed at me. "Did your body double take them?"

I held up my hands. "I can't even stand right now. I've been in this chair the whole time."

"Janin," Vanna said.

"Janin?" Sora's voice rose. "You let *Janin* in on your assignment and not me?"

"I needed someone to bring my sub to me." Vanna shot me a look. "By the way, twisting your ankle really messed things up."

"I don't think I'm your problem right now," I said.

"This just shows you weren't ready," Sora said. "If you'd done your research, you would have known that Janin has a criminal record under another identity. Being your tutor was a cover so I could investigate Janin."

"I thought being a maid was your cover," I said.

"Double cover," Vanna and Sora said at the same time.

Vanna shook her head. "That woman knows every room in this palace. It was her idea to meet in the butler's office."

"She's been dating the butler for two months now!" Sora said.

Vanna paused. "Really? She's, like, twenty years older than him. But I guess she's in good shape . . ."

87

"FOCUS," Sora said. "I'll cover the hall."

"And I'll get the west wing," Vanna said. "Of course she waited until after our identities switched."

"Hey!" I waved my arms. "Stop."

Vanna and Sora stared down at me. For being spies, they really took a roundabout way to solve a simple problem. Vanna might hope to work for an elite government agency, but I happened to have access to a magical agency that knew every single thing the royals did. When I'd tried on the tiaras, Ferdinand told me that Façade tracked royal valuables. The crown jewels would have to be in that system. I fumbled around for my manual and held it up. "There's a Façade application that traces all the royals' valuables. If I show it to you, you have to promise not to tell anyone. I'm not sure you're supposed to know."

Vanna lunged for the manual. I hid it behind my back. "Not yet," I said. "When you do your Princess Progress Report, say I'm the best sub you've ever had, that I'm totally trustworthy and have great instincts, and, let's see, that I should be able to do whatever I want at the agency."

Sora gave me an appraising look. "I don't know what agency you work for, but I'd love to hire you."

"Yes! Deal," Vanna said. "Now hurry."

I clicked around on the manual until I found the application. There was a long list of items, but one click in the search engine and the Kamigano crown jewels popped right up. A satellite shot of the palace with a blinking red dot showed the jewels were out in the garden, stationary.

"They aren't moving," I said.

"Not yet, at least. She's probably figuring out her getaway," Sora said.

Vanna growled. "I know you're antiviolence, Sora, but right now I could—"

"Take it," I said, holding out my manual to Vanna. "You and Sora can use the radar to keep tabs on Janin. Just . . . please please please don't drop it. Or tell anyone I let you use my manual. I could lose my job." And if I was going to lose my job, I hoped it would be for a nobler cause than chasing after Janin.

Vanna and Sora bolted out of the office, leaving me alone, in a wheelchair, with no idea where I was or what I was supposed to do. I couldn't summon my bubble without my manual. I couldn't leave without my manual, either. So I did what any normal teenager would do in my situation.

I raided the mini-fridge. And glory hallelujah! The butler had a sweet tooth. I found a candy bar—the brand was foreign, but these people knew their nougat—and set my feet up on the desk. It wasn't quite as relaxing as Vanna's bed, but it was still a lot better than wheeling around with a jewel thief. Plus, I was following Ferdinand's advice. You didn't have to make a big wave to start a ripple. I just handed over my manual and let the princess do the work. Delegation.

Vanna returned in ten minutes, panting. "We got Janin. Just barely. She'd made a deal with my father's helicopter pilot—he already had clearance, and in the confusion, no one seemed to notice that there wasn't a royal in there. But

Sora jumped onto the landing skid just as they were taking off and punched the pilot and handcuffed Janin . . . I think at the same time. So anyway, the jewels are safe, but this agency I've been trying to get into thinks I need more time. Obviously, I failed."

"I've thought I failed a million times, and things usually end up working out for the best. Get some more training from Sora—she's the real deal—and you'll make it."

Vanna drummed her fingers against the door. "I hope. And when I do, I might need to call you in as a decoy again. After I give you the greatest PPR of all time, of course." She tossed me my manual. "Thanks for that. I guess I'll go find my parents now and explain how my ankle miraculously recovered."

"Hey, Vanna?" I said. "You should tell your parents that you want to work for the government."

She rolled her eyes. "So they can tell me no? If they even listen in the first place. No, thanks."

"But they *might* say yes. And being a royal doesn't have to hurt you—it can help you. Look at what you were able to do today with a sub. You might be able to find a role with your government that no one else can fill but you. Think about it."

"I will." Vanna snapped her fingers. "Oh, and you got a text or something on that manual thing while I was using it. I hope I didn't accidentally erase it."

When Vanna left, I took an extra minute to finish off the candy bar and decompress. This had been the most action-packed sub job yet, and I loved it. Being on the job made it hard to think about what I could lose if I crossed Façade. What if I could find a way to keep my job and still make changes? Wouldn't that be awesome? I'd love to see what other spy training Vanna had in store.

I brushed my hands on my jeans and opened the new e-mail. It was not a message I'd been expecting.

The Façade Agency
Cordially invites you to
the Council Restructuring Declaration
An open discussion forum and celebratory reception
will immediately follow the announcement.
Invitation required for admission

Awesome. Maybe that's what Meredith had been doing at Façade—pulling strings to get me an official invitation to her promotion. I scrolled through my manual to my bubble app, and my personal magical orb poured right out. I lifted myself out of the wheelchair and hopped inside.

"Hello, Desi," Daisy chirped. "Your destination is set at HOME."

There were crutches conveniently perched next to my fluffy red chair. Daisy was the best. Too bad she hadn't thrown in an energy bar to follow up that chocolate I'd swiped. I was going to need the extra jolt before this meeting.

"Change my destination to Façade, Daisy. I need to go back to Façade."

Chapter

10

I did a little research while Daisy whisked me over to Façade. The exclusive guest list included a sprinkling of agents and only a very select number of Level Threes. In fact, subs had never been invited to a restructuring event. There was a thread going on in the chat room, filled with speculation about why we were invited. The theories ranged from promotions to a new agency branch, but no one seemed to know for sure. The big mystery was the open discussion forum. They hadn't held such a meeting in decades. And I was barely a Level Three. Was this all Meredith's doing, or did Genevieve want me there for another reason?

Daisy dropped me off smack in the crowded dining area

of Dorshire Hall. Nearly every one of the dozens of onlookers had multicolored hair, a sign that they were agents or council members. Or another department, I guess. I didn't know which employees were granted Hair-Dye Rights. There were more men then I'd ever seen here as well—some council members I recognized from my trial with the Court of Royal Appeals, but others were undoubtedly agents who worked for Specter.

In the sea of rainbow dos, I spotted Reed's dark hair and tall frame. He looked dazed as he peered up at the gallery of Façade historical portraits sloping up the vaulted ceiling. I'm sure I looked the same way when I saw those paintings the first time Genevieve shared some of Façade's history with me. But looking at the pictures now, I couldn't help but be cynical. Which one of those employees invented sub-sanitation? Who decided that subs shouldn't be friends? Why was magic only accessible to royals?

Reed spotted me and gave a quick nod. Now would actually be a perfect time for us to finish our talk—it was not like anyone would pay attention to our conversation with so much going on.

But before I could make my way over to Reed, Meredith sidled up to me and threw an arm over my shoulder. I swayed a little, catching myself on my crutches. Her face looked scary. She was smiling—like, *grinning*—and she had these lines . . . laugh lines? Wow. This was Meredith. Happy. "Darling! You're here. Almost in one piece."

"Accident in Kamigano."

"Yes, do stop and see Ferdinand about that before you go. He has a special first-aid kit that should help. And be more careful!"

I shifted my weight. "This saved me a sub spotting, if you must know."

"Oh, let's not talk about that now." Meredith dropped her arm and stood up on her tippy toes, taking in the growing mass of people. "Can you believe you got an invite?"

"No, I can't. Is this your doing?"

"I suggested you, yes, but Genevieve said she already had you in mind. She specifically said she wanted you to see me advance. Isn't she lovely?"

"Lovely." Something told me Genevieve wanted me here for other reasons. Maybe to keep her eye on me, or to remind me how powerful Façade was. She was a nice person, yes, and I was glad she was the head of Façade. But you don't get where she is without being a little conniving, too. "But I'm still not exactly sure what this invite is for."

Meredith lowered her voice. "Well, the first part is my promotion, of course, although no one else knows that's happening. And the open discussion forum, well, I probably shouldn't tell you too much, but they're introducing a program where appointed Level Three subs will have a direct voice during select council meetings."

"A voice? Like, we can give our opinions?" If this was true, then I didn't need to worry about recruiting Reed anymore, or using my new special spy skills here at Façade. I didn't need to worry about anything. If we had a voice in the agency, we could discuss sub sanitization and magic stealing. Write a petition! And maybe brainstorm ways to better prepare subs for jobs and how to fully realize their MP. Oh, maybe they could start a sort of mentor program, so girls aren't just thrown into jobs. Or job shadowing, like take-your-sub-hopeful-to-work day.

I shook my head. There were so many questions to ask, I couldn't even settle on one thing. "I can't even . . . This is just . . ."

"I know. You're a lucky girl, Desi." Her smile faltered, and her voice took on its usual businesslike nature. "Now, when we're in this meeting, please wait until it is your turn to talk. You're still my client, and thus a reflection of me, and with my new promotion I would really appreciate it—"

"—If I didn't mess this up. I got it."

"We'll see about that."

"Yoo-hoo! Meredith!" Lilith pushed through the throngs of people, her lavender hair bouncing along with the rest of her. "Oh, and Desi. Lovely wardrobe choice, especially your T-shirt. ON A ROLL? So very . . . down home."

"Lilith, I'm so glad you're here," Meredith said.

"Yes, well, I must say I'm surprised to see you two showed. Did you come to mingle until the invited guests entered? I can let you know how the meeting goes, if you like. All this administrative business might bore you, of course, but—"

"Don't worry about us." Meredith's grin was back at full throttle. "Desi and I received our invitations ages ago."

Lilith's eyes bugged out. "Surely you don't mean you're *attending* the council meeting."

"Oh, we're doing more than attending. Meredith is about to—" Meredith grabbed my arm to shut me up. I guess she wanted Lilith to learn the news when everyone else did.

A loud boom filled the hall, and we all turned around. The doors to the conference room opened. Genevieve stood in the doorway, dressed in a slim black skirt and bright red blouse, her rainbow-colored hair arranged in a neat coif. She gave a slight nod, and a handful of people followed her into the room. That's power. No words needed—one nod.

"Well, this should be quick," Lilith said. "I have it on good authority that Genevieve isn't retiring, and so there won't be anyone moving up to council head. No changes, no promotions. This meeting is just to dispel rumors."

"If that's what you want to believe," I said. Meredith elbowed me again. Why was she being so quiet? She should rub her promotion right in Lilith's face.

Lilith scowled. "You two are just . . . so . . . common."

"I guess we'll find out what's happening together." Meredith wiggled her fingers at Lilith. "Ta-ta, darling."

Lilith shot us one more cutting look and charged for the doors. I gave Meredith's hand a quick squeeze. "Save me a seat. I'll be there in a second. Good luck."

"One thing I've learned in this business, it's not about luck." She squared her shoulders and marched through the doorway.

Only a small percentage of the congregation actually

walked into the conference room. Reed waited for me at the entrance. "Hey, what happened to your ankle?"

"Had a run-in with a bridge, and the bridge won. Have you been at Façade the whole time?"

"Yeah, Sergei finally gave me the grand tour. Can you believe this place?" Reed's eyes shone. "It's the perfect opportunity to visit Façade. Specter has a conference center, but Dorshire Hall is the stuff of legend. My parents are going to be blown away. *They* weren't even invited to this meeting. Do you know how elite this is?"

"Yeah, yeah. The royal treatment," I said, then added under my breath, "once again."

Of course he didn't mention the big news I'd dumped on him. He was under the spell of Façade's beauty. And what did that all matter now? We were about to meet with the council to discuss the framework of the agency. Anything that was wrong before could be fixed with a mature, diplomatic discussion.

The doors to the conference room were closing. "We better hurry," I said. "I want some time to think about what I'm going to say to the council."

Reed's forehead wrinkled. "But nothing about what you said to me earlier, right?"

I paused. "What if I did?"

"I just mean . . . this is our first meeting. You might not want to, you know, get too involved."

Sometimes, Reed's cuteness made me forget his annoying quirks. Like his know-it-all-ness. Too involved? I was already sinking in magical quicksand. This meeting was the stick that would pull me out. "You can be really clueless, you know that, Reed?"

"I am not the one who's acting clueless."

"What are you saying?"

"Nothing, just . . . I'm trying to look out for you. I'm sure you believe what you said, but I'm saying this because I really care—"

"Desi! Over here!" Meredith waved at us from across the vast room. Sergei was next to her, his arm casually draped around her chair. I hurried over to them, Reed on my heels. How could Reed be so bossy one minute and say that he cared the next? What a mix of emotions. I would just have to show him that I was right about Façade when I addressed the council—and the fifty other people in the room.

It was a long march across the conference room to Meredith. You could fit the population of a small country around the table alone.

Within a minute, the room went quiet, like someone had gradually turned down the volume on a radio dial. Genevieve rose from her seat. She nodded at the silver-haired man on her left, who stood and nodded to the next person, and the next, until the twelve council members formed a silent wall in front of the large congregation.

"Everyone may be seated." Genevieve smiled. "I would officially like to call this meeting to order."

Chapter

11

The room dimmed to a subdued purple. A halo of light illuminated Genevieve as she spread her arms wide. "As you well know, Façade was first established in the year 1483, under the direction of Beatrix the Bold. Within this newly formed institution, Beatrix established a council of six females, including three of her sisters. The initial goal of the agency was to protect female royalty. Beatrix also controlled the royals' access to magic through the Charm Treaty of 1491. Changes have been made since that first meeting. The first man was sworn into the council two hundred years ago. The Rouge formula was expanded to an extensive royal makeup line, which now provides twenty-five percent of our profits. And of course, the council number grew to twelve. Council meetings have been conducted in this room for centuries, and it is very rare indeed for the invite list to be so expansive. So why are you here?"

No one moved. No one seemed to breathe.

"First off, let me begin by dispelling a rumor. I am not retiring."

The collective breath was let out. Murmurs began. Meredith squeezed my hand. Her fingers were icicles, and her mouth was frozen in a tight line. I couldn't imagine what this moment must have been like for her, knowing that everything in her life was about to change.

Lilith smirked at me from across the table. I couldn't wait to see her expression in just a few more minutes.

"As such, we are not appointing a new head of council today. But I have decided to make a few changes, and that is why I've asked you all here." Genevieve held up her pointer finger. "Number one involves an increase in our ranks. I would like the reception for our thirteenth council member to be warm and welcoming."

News of a thirteenth council member hit the audience with a physical force. The promotion now seemed possible to everyone. Foam was going to drip from Lilith's mouth if Genevieve didn't move faster.

A screen slid down from the ceiling behind Genevieve, displaying the number thirteen and a question mark. "This agent has been vital to our agency, and now it is time for her to use her background to serve the council," Genevieve began. "She has overcome many obstacles, both in her professional and personal life, but always has been devoted to her career. We look forward to her continued devotion as we create a new role for her. What her duties will be remains to be seen, but for now, please join me in welcoming the newest and youngest member to the Façade council. Meredith Pouffinski, please stand."

Meredith's image filled the screen. There was a shocked silence as Meredith's chair scraped against the floor and she rose to her full four feet eleven inches. A serene smile played on her lips, but I could see her foot jiggling under the table. After the pause, the room burst into applause, all except for Lilith, who folded her arms purposefully across her chest. Meredith nodded at the audience, enjoying a moment she'd probably hoped for her whole life.

I wondered if she would text her prince about this. I wondered if she said *anything* to him anymore.

Genevieve raised a hand and the room quieted again. The screen went dark.

"I realize this news is a bit shocking, but predictability is for the predictable. Meredith will be inducted to the council in a private ceremony later today, but a celebratory feast will be served by the Dorshire chef immediately after this meeting. I hope you will congratulate Meredith on her new position. Thank you, Meredith."

Meredith took her seat. If she was aware that every single person in the room was staring at her with envy, she didn't show it.

"There is one more item of business to attend to," Genevieve continued. "You'll also notice we have quite a few younger Façade employees here today. I've invited a select number of Level Three substitutes to join us because of their exemplary performance in the field. I'll invite you all to stand now."

Five subs besides myself stood—three boys including Reed, and two other girls. The boys weren't boys so much as men . . . easily in their early twenties, with an effortless preppy appeal. The larger girl sub was around their age also, w ith beautiful brown skin and dark curly hair. Which left the girl standing next to Lilith. She was waiflike, probably two or three years older than me. I smiled, and she stared at me. No smile. So maybe Lilith had already made this girl aware of who I was.

"Thank you. You may be seated. These subs are the future of Façade. They may serve on this very council some- day. They may even hold my job. One of our new initiatives is a substitute ambassadorship. For a portion of each council meeting, we will invite one boy and one girl to attend as a representative for substitutes, or surrogates. They may offer any suggestions, talk about successes or even grievances. After all, subs are our eyes and ears in the field."

Genevieve's speech gave me the goose bumps. Today was going to go down in Façade history, and I was a part of it!

"To witness the effectiveness of this new program, I've asked Isabel and Gregory to be our first substitute spokespeo- ple. Again, I cannot stress how progressively groundbreaking this moment is." She motioned to one of the boys. "Gregory, if you will?"

I felt a pang of disappointment that I wouldn't be able to address the council today, but part of being democratic was giving everyone a turn to speak. I'd also have more time to prepare my arguments. Maybe one of these subs would even say something similar to my concerns and I could build on that.

Gregory stood. His stature was large and commanding. His voice boomed. "Thank you for this honor, Genevieve. There is something of grave importance I'd like to address. Something that has weighed heavily on my heart. Something to do with usage of magic and cosmetics."

I almost yelled, "Amen!" Gregory was my man. Gregory was going to make my job so much easier. It was totally obvious that too much magic was wasted on the makeup. Thank goodness I had Gregory to get the ball rolling.

"Specter has been part of this agency for centuries now. And as such, our needs have been overlooked. Where is the *male* makeup line?" Gregory pumped his fist into the air. "Where are the antiaging serums specifically triggered to the contours of a *man's* face? Where are the soothing after-shaves? The women are given makeup that makes them look fifteen years younger, while we still walk around with receding hairlines! Where is the justice in *that?*"

The crowd nodded thoughtfully, like male makeup was a viable topic of discussion. Gregory! You're kidding me. Go glob on some concealer if you're worried about wrinkles. Or better yet, go take on the appearance of a handsome prince.

I couldn't believe that I worked for an agency where a guy like this was actually being taken seriously. He could have asked for new vending machines in the lobby and been more helpful. At least then I could go chug a Mountain Dew to calm my nerves.

Genevieve tapped a pen to her mouth. "I'm so sorry the agency has been blind to your needs, Gregory. This is an issue we clearly need to address." Genevieve turned to a blue-haired woman to her left. "Esmeralda, you're over that. I want a male-cosmetic sub committee organized stat." She beamed. "See? This is how we progress as an institution."

The room broke into applause. Sergei crossed the room and gave Gregory a gruff hug. I caught Reed's eye and he shrugged. I knew him well enough to know he thought this was stupid too. At least I wasn't the only sane person in the room.

"Now, Isabel, what would you like to add to the conversation?" Genevieve asked.

Isabel was already putting on some lipstick. Lilith reached over and fluffed her hair and they gave each other a hug before Isabel stood and flashed a bright smile to the crowd. "I would not change a thing about Façade. The tradition our foremothers set for us is respectable, honorable, wise, and pragmatic."

I snuck a glance at Lilith. She was mouthing the words with Isabel.

I slumped back in my seat. My dreams of committees and proposals were already melting away. If I wanted to make any changes here, it wasn't going to be by convincing a large group of people that something they'd done for generations was wrong. Especially when they had things like boy blush to worry about.

Isabel was still going. ". . . I appreciate the venerable traditions of sovereigns and surrogates past, and think those relationships should continue into the ages. Let us not forget, we work for monarchs, for the elite, the exalted, and the privileged. We must not lose our credibility by adapting the ideals of . . ." She paused, making a face. "Democracy. We have a wonderful institution here. I elect we keep Façade exactly the way it is. Thank you."

Lilith burst into applause. The crowd followed with polite clapping. Genevieve cleared her throat. "Well, thank you for those heartfelt adulations. Glad to hear you support Façade so fervently. A lovely note to end on, I believe. Ambassadors, you know the framework for future meetings, and you will be contacted when it's time for you to address the council. This section of the meeting will now close so we might celebrate our newest member. Please, enjoy the music and food, and thank you all for your hard work at Façade!"

Well, that was a royal waste of time. I turned to tell Meredith this, along with a bunch of other grievances, but she was already standing, already being whisked away by the congratulatory masses. She was glowing and laughing and . . . happy. It was the happiest I'd seen her at work, almost as happy as she was with her prince. I sighed. Great. That wasn't something I could mess with, not today. Yet another important topic to save for another time. I might explode with all the save-upiness inside me.

The crowd spilled into Dorshire Hall. Banquet tables and bouquets of fresh flowers added more appeal to the eloquent space. I set my sights on the dessert table. At least they would have cream puffs. Cream puffs would never leave me. Cream puffs would never promise a revolution and then provide a student council speech. They may be puffy, but they are true to what they are.

I reached the table and took in the petit fours, the iced tiara cookies, the macaroons. There weren't any cream puffs. The one thing I wanted, and Façade couldn't deliver. Typical. I settled for an éclair. An éclair and a fleeting chance that anything at Façade would ever change.

A brass band jammed in the corner as waiters circled with appetizers. Agents mingled with council members, who chatted with people I'd never seen before, serving on committees I'd never heard of. If this many people were at an "exclusive" event, it made me wonder how big Façade really was. Meredith's promotion was a *very* big deal. And if she was a big deal now, was she still going to have time for me? If I didn't have Meredith on my side, who did I have?

The other Level Threes stood in a circle near the salad bar. Reed caught my eye and nodded me over. Oh, goodie. Maybe Gregory would share ideas on how to save his manly cuticles. And I wasn't too eager to talk to Reed, either, since our conversations left me feeling so sweet and sour. And Lilith's little prodigy . . . no thanks. Still, I didn't know these other subs. Maybe one would turn to me and say, "You know what I was just thinking, Desi? That whole magic-stealing thing is a bummer. Let's lobby against that, K?"

Gregory was receiving compliments on his moving cosmetics speech. I leaned back on my crutches and tried to eat my éclair in silence, but when he started to compare himself to some of the American founding fathers, I snorted.

Gregory squinted at me. "Is there a problem?"

I swallowed the rest of my éclair and licked my fingers. "No. I mean, its *just* makeup. Not life or death."

"Do you know how hard it is to get in character for a self-confident prince like Harry when I don't *feel* confident underneath? Do you?"

"Harry?" I asked. "Prince Harry? Of England? You sub for him?"

"I'm his Match. And as such, I deserve the same respect and privileges afforded our agents."

"You're still talking about makeup, right?" I asked.

Reed squeezed my elbow and whispered, "Desi, careful—"

I shook him off. "No, I'm just saying, I'm all for equality, but you're thinking small potatoes."

"And what potatoes would you have in mind?" Gregory sneered.

"What about where the magic for that makeup comes from?" I asked.

The older girl flipped her dark hair. "Don't tell me you're going to go off on animal testing. It doesn't hurt the organisms to take magic, you know."

The group stared at me like I was a creature from one of Kylee's favorite movies. Reed looked at his feet. So they all bought the same story—extra magic came from organic material. None of them knew the harsh truth. And if I told them, would they believe me? Doubt it. They all had a great job. Why question that?

"Never mind," I grumbled.

"And, I'm sorry, but how long have you been a sub?" Gregory asked. "I don't mean to be obtuse, but you're obviously very young and inexperienced. So why are you here? I'm curious."

Because I know secrets you don't. "I don't know. I just am."

"Are you doubting Genevieve?" Reed cut in.

Gregory barked a laugh. "Of course not."

"Well, Desi obviously must be very talented and smart if she's gotten so far so fast. So maybe we should give her some respect."

"How long have you been here?" Isabel asked.

"Almost six months," I said.

"Wow," Gregory said. They stood there, staring at me, trying to figure out what made me so special.

It was in that moment that I made up my mind. I could either be a part of the problem, or I could be a part of the solution. I had tried to be rational, tried to play by the rules, and it just wasn't working. I could wait until it was my turn to address the council as a substitute ambassador, but who was to say they would listen to me? I mean, they already KNEW about sub-sanitation; they were the ones who invented it. No, I needed to take some action myself.

Now was the time to make a *real* impact. "I have to go." I hobbled away, out of Dorshire, away from all the confusion. There were footsteps behind me, but I didn't look back. I didn't want to talk to anyone. I took a painful hop down each stair, trying not to let the ankle slow down my resolve. I was starting to form a plan now and wouldn't have much time to execute it.

"Desi!" Reed caught up to me easily, his hand light on my shoulder.

"What do you want?" I asked.

"Why are you so mad?"

"I'm not."

"You are. Here, let me help." He swooped me up into his arms and stuck my crutches on top of me. I didn't even have time to object—he had me down the stairs and seated on a bench before I knew it. My skin was all tingly from his touch. He kneeled down in front of me and brushed a hair away from my face. "Now. Is this about that crazy stolen magic story?"

I flinched. Story? He made it sound like I'd wiggled my way into this little club. I didn't ask for any of this. I was actually really happy at Level One, trying to make little impacts in my clients' lives, not worrying about ambassador meetings and Matching and power. Reed didn't get that because he was a legacy. Born and bred to be a part of Façade. He'd lived with this his whole life and had never had cause to question.

"It wasn't a story," I said.

"Okay. But what I'm really concerned about right now is how upset you are."

I buried my face in my hands. He might think I was nuts, but he also cared about me, or at least cared if I was upset. He'd defended me in front of all those people, not worrying if he looked crazy by association.

Who could blame him for thinking I was making up my "story"? The sub-sanitation room is really one of those things you have to see to believe. Which meant I needed to include Reed on my plan. I was going to the sub-sanitation room. Right now. Meredith had a special key to get in, but Reed said that I could program my manual to get anywhere into Façade. Why not there? And once he saw those glowing vials filled with stolen magic, he would *have* to believe me.

"Hey, you want to go explore Façade some more?" I asked. "I could show you some places Sergei didn't."

"Can't. Sergei just sent me an urgent job." He smiled and held up his manual. "Another time, though?"

"Yeah. Another time."

Reed reached over and gave my hand a little squeeze. "Be careful out there."

My hand was still buzzing minutes after he left. Stupid hand. Didn't matter who Reed was or how I felt about him in Sproutville. Here, he was important, and here he didn't want to listen to me. And although that realization was painful, it didn't change what I needed to do.

Infiltrate Façade.

Chapter

12

$\mathcal{A}$s I limped through Façade's corridors, I devised DBIF: TBP, short for Desi Bascomb Infiltrates Façade: The Battle Plan.

1. Find a map of Façade.
2. Get into the sub-sanitation room.
3. Find a former sub's magic.
4. Return/restore that sub's magic.

The problems with that plan:

1. Façade: Even if I managed to find a map, I still wouldn't have an invisibility cloak to hide me. I couldn't

cover all of my tracks. And if surveillance went back to monitor where I had been, they could document my every move.

2. Room: There is a special key that I didn't have. There was an application that I needed to somehow access and *hope* even worked.

3. Magic: When Meredith showed me the Wall o' Magic, there were thousands of vessels, and there could be much more stored somewhere else. To just pick up one vessel and know who originally owned that magic was not going to be easy. Forget easy. Impossible.

4. Return: And if I did figure out who owned that magic, I had to return it without Façade knowing and somehow make that sub magical again.

To put it optimistically, I was doomed.

But Vanna's tenacity had inspired me to take the risk. I could get in trouble. I could lose my job. I could be sub sanitized. And that's if Façade was feeling kind. But that meeting was the last straw. I couldn't know what I knew and pretend that I didn't.

First stop was the lobby, where Meredith said Ferdinand could somehow help with my injuries. It took forever to get there with my crutches. When I finally reached the front desk, I was out of breath. "Hi, Ferdinand!" I wheezed.

He cleared his throat. "What happened to your ankle?"

"Just another subbing escapade. Meredith said you might be able to help with that?"

"Yes. And if there's anything else, you'll need to sign in since you're here alone."

"Oh, really?" Man, that's probably why Meredith wanted me to come down here first, so I wasn't sneaking around Façade without documentation. I scribbled my name, fudging my entry time by a few minutes. There was a space asking my reason for visiting. Somehow, sabotage didn't seem like a good thing to write down. Then I had a genius idea, something that might just solve the next glitch in my plan. I wrote *Broken manual.*

Ferdinand took the clipboard from me and glanced up. "You'll want to head over to Central Command to get that manual fixed. Do you know where to go?"

I scratched my head. "Um, kind of? Do you have a map of Façade?" A map that would also have directions to the sub-sanitation room hidden somewhere deep in the belly of the agency.

"A map? So anyone could waltz in and wander anywhere they like? No maps."

I twirled a piece a hair around my finger, hoping Ferdinand didn't notice my hand shaking. "Oh. Sorry. I just get lost super easy."

He pointed to the hallway on the right. "Go down there. Central Command is on the left. And," he lowered his voice. "If you *really* need a map, Hank would be the one to ask. But I didn't tell you that."

"Tell me what?" I asked innocently.

"As far as your injury goes." Ferdinand opened a drawer and took out a jar of loose powder. "Let me see your ankle."

He walked around the receptionist desk and knelt down in front of me, his knees creaking. One shake of the sheer powder and I could physically feel the swelling in my ankle leave. "Oh, my gosh," I said.

"Anywhere else?" he asked.

I motioned to my knee. Another shake and I was just like the Tin Man after a few drops of oil. I dropped the crutches and tested my foot. Fine. Better than fine. Man, I was so glad Ferdinand was the one working the reception desk and not one of Lilith's drones—they might have swapped the powder with some wart potion.

"They make makeup that can heal injuries," I said.

"In the testing stages. I hear it can cause rapid hair growth, so be careful with that."

"Ferdinand, they have the power to *heal*, and they're not using it on non-royals, too?" My voice was almost shrill.

He gave me a stern look. "I believe that the power was just used on you, and you're not royalty. Now, didn't you have a manual to fix?"

"Oh, yeah." I took a few more hesitant steps, in shock of my newfound mobility and the fact that Façade had another trick that should be mass-produced for the greater good. They probably only used that powder on princess hangnails. "Thank you, Ferdinand. Seriously, you're the best."

He gave me a grandfatherly wink and waved me away.

I pasted a smile on my face and skipped down the hall, doing my best to look like a carefree little sub with nothing wrong but a glitched manual. Everything had worked so far. The hard stuff was ahead.

When I got to Central Command, I stood in the doorway and watched the activity for a minute. This was the mission control of Façade. One screen monitored magical activity; another, bubble-flight radars; and computers whirred with mysterious information. Lilith once described the folks here as "technomagical," the science geeks of Façade.

I spotted Hank, the hipster computer boy who had first given me my manual. He grinned when he noticed me. "Desi Bascomb. You just can't get enough of me, can you?"

I felt heat rise in my cheeks. Hank was a few years older than me, and although I knew he was only joking around, I still didn't quite know how to respond to guys like that. Reed was really the only boy I'd ever been able to be myself around. And Karl. Who was really Reed subbing for Karl. "Hi, Hank. I have a little problem with my manual. I know you're the one to fix it."

"Sure." Another tech person whisked past us. The room was always in such a frenzy, I wondered how they didn't leave every day with a huge headache. Or suffer a caffeine overdose—the coffee center was used more frequently than the computers. "What's up?"

"Sometimes the screen just dies on me."

Hank took my manual and started punching buttons. "Looks fine to me."

"Yeah, it usually is, but it doesn't always work. Totally random."

"Did you try rebooting it?"

"No." I smiled at him. "See, I knew it was something little. Sorry to waste your time."

"Time well spent." Hank handed back the manual. I turned as if to leave, then paused like I'd just had a thought. "Hey, since I'm here, can you make sure all the updates and applications are current and stuff?"

"You want me to trick it out?" he asked, a glimmer of mischief in his eyes.

"Sure. I don't know if there are updates that need to be added now that I'm Level Three. And . . ." I paused, my heart pounding. "Another sub told me there is some key app? And I heard there was a map for Façade? I'm always losing my way around here, and I feel stupid every time I have to ask for help."

Hank motioned me over to his table of computers. He tapped on his keyboard at lightning speed. "So don't tell anyone I'm doing this, but I figure with your quick advancements, the council is in love with you anyway and just hasn't gotten around to getting you updated."

"Right," I said, trying to hide the urgency in my voice. The flashing lights and loud noise around us was not calming my nerves. And maybe I was just being paranoid, but I swear everyone kept looking at me, almost like they knew what I was planning to do.

"Map is on there. We don't get GPS in the building, so it can't show you where you are, just a general overview."

"Good. The map will still help." Ugh, I was sweating.

Sweating was so not stealth! "You know, in case I ever get lost."

"So for the door app, you just press the key button and locate the door you're trying to access. A green light appears, and you cover the doorknob with the manual. It should unlock. And if you have another manual there, you're more likely to get in. They combine power."

"Kind of like the muting application," I said.

Hank looked up at me appraisingly. "You know about that app?"

Whoops. I licked my lips.

He stood so that we were super close. I could just see his dark blue eyes under his FREE THE PEOPLE hat. "You're manual wasn't busted, was it?"

I avoided his gaze, which I learned during my Vanna training was a sure sign of deceit, but I *was* lying, so . . . "It really was, you know, random."

Hank laughed. "Now I see how you moved up so fast." Something on his computer beeped. He plugged a cord from his computer into my manual, then handed it back to me. "Updated. Be smart with it."

"Thanks." I tried to keep the relief out of my voice. Two obstacles down. "I'll see you around."

"Yeah, stop by again," Hank said. "Don't be one of those snobby magical types who won't mix with the techno geeks."

"Never."

A red light flashed on the MP meter, the radar that

detected magic, and Hank hurried over to the screen. "Take care, Desi!" he called.

See? There were a lot of cool people working at Façade. Hopefully, I didn't do something that brought the whole agency down and made someone like Hank lose his job. I had a feeling he wouldn't be quite as content working the Genius Bar at the Apple store.

Once outside of Central, I pulled up the map application. Not having a GPS actually worked to my advantage—if I couldn't see where I was, Façade might not be able to, either. At least not from a satellite. There were, of course, security cameras all over. I knew that I was going to get caught on film, so I had to figure out a believable reason for being in sub-sanitation.

The room didn't appear on the map, but there was a "sub-questioning" room that was far removed from anything else in the building. This had to be it. I started down the twisty maze that made up Façade. I vaguely remembered some of the hallways I walked through during my last venture here, how the decor became more sparse, with only an occasional medieval tapestry to lend any cheer. Why waste time or money on decoration when most people who made it this far didn't remember Façade five minutes later anyway?

And then I saw the door—white with an old-fashioned handle—and I knew I was in the right place. Although there was nothing *right* about what was behind that door.

Nothing right at all.

Chapter
I3

I was back to sweaty hands (and fingers) as I scrolled through the new manual apps, Someone could show up at any minute. When I pressed the key application button, the screen read INPUT DOOR. I typed in "sub-questioning" and the screen read DOOR NOT RECOGNIZED. I typed in "sub-sanitation" and the screen read DOOR NOT RECOGNIZED. I tweaked the name, thought of ten different variations, but the screen never registered. Most of these doors were electronic—this one required that old-fashioned key Meredith carried around her neck.

Old-fashioned keys had old-fashioned locks. And locks could be picked. Just ask Vanna.

My hair was twisted in front with a little bobby pin. I plucked the pin out of my hair and bent it straight. The lock was fairly easy to undo—just a little digging with the pin, and *click!* I tried the handle. The door opened to darkness.

I didn't step through right away. There could be a laser alarm or . . . motion-activated blow darts, or Genevieve. Her office was secretly hidden next door. I wadded my ON A ROLL T-shirt into a ball, ignoring the chill in my thin tank top, and threw the shirt into the room. No sirens went off. Nothing happened. I took a hesitant step inside, and then another, closing the door behind me.

The space was empty except for a few white lab tables on the spotless floor. I couldn't remember which wall was magical, so I tiptoed around the perimeter of the room, tapping each wall twice. On the third wall, the white exterior rolled away, revealing rows and rows of built-in shelves holding hundreds of colorful jars. The magical storage vessels.

Now. Which one should I take? Maybe I could find Fake McKenzie's magic, the girl I'd watched in the Idaho beauty pageant during Level Two. She'd been a little too enthusiastic and done better in the pageant than instructed, leading to a quick memory wash in this very room. My experience as a Watcher for Fake McKenzie was the reason I'd started to doubt Façade in the first place. But I didn't even know the girl's first name. And the shelves were endless. So much magic.

I analyzed the shelves more closely, and my heart sank. Each vial swirled with colors and a long label with names wrapped around the tube. Gretchen Uzuri Barbara Olga Soo Maria . . . Great. The magic was *mixed*. I couldn't just grab a container and give one girl her magic back. Each vial held the potential of dozens.

And not like it mattered, because each vial had a computerized security system. A code needed to be entered to remove the containers. No wonder it was so easy to get into this room—even if I knew about that hidden wall, I couldn't touch anything there.

My hope had been a façade, too.

I slumped down on the ground and tucked my newly healed knee underneath me. The tears came so fast, I didn't bother to wipe them away. I couldn't give back magic. Why did I ever think I could? I thought I could just break down this wall and everything would be restored, like I was someone super-talented, like Vanna. I was one regular person. One person against a centuries-old institution.

"Please tell me you aren't having a pity party."

I looked up. Meredith leaned against one of the white lab tables.

"Am I going to be in trouble?" I asked in a small, pitiful voice.

"Not *in* trouble. But you most certainly *are* trouble. And please don't take that as a compliment and go tattoo it on your arm or anything." Meredith knelt down next to me, gently brushing a hair away from my face. "Are you trying to save the world again?"

Another sob burst out of me, and I wiped away snot

with the back of my hand. Having Meredith mad at me was easier than having her sympathy. Softness from her was such a rarity that I knew I must be completely hopeless if she was pulling that deep emotion out now.

"I did the same thing, you know," she whispered.

"What, got snot all over yourself?"

"No." She handed me a tissue. "I came here."

I wiped my eyes. "To the sanitation room?"

"No one ever saw me. I've never told anyone about my field trip."

My master plan seemed so optimistically foolish now. Maybe I'd been too confident, too full of myself.

"Were you trying to . . . trying to . . ." I couldn't say out loud what I had tried to do.

Meredith ignored the question. "Did you know they used to bring the Watcher along when the sub hopeful was sanitized? I don't know why—I think we were supposed to serve as witnesses. I had one hopeful that really got to me. Poor girl was on the ground, pleading for another chance. Then one makeup application and she was smiling at me like we'd never met." She shook her head. "Her name was Caprice. She was from Florence, in Italy. She didn't pass because she was too nice. Didn't have an edge."

"She lost her power because she was *nice?*" I asked.

"I think about her a lot," Meredith continued. "She acts and waits tables in Los Angeles now. She's a lousy actress, but she would have been a good sub. If she had the training. If she had some time. If the agency didn't try to fit all these different-shaped pegs into their magical square holes. They sold her short, but they did value Caprice's magic enough to remove and recycle."

I let out a humorless laugh. "I was hoping I could find Fake McKenzie's magic, the girl I watched in Celeste's beauty pageant. I wanted to see what would happen if she had magic back."

"That wouldn't be good. Being here isn't a good idea, either." Meredith stared straight ahead. She chewed on her bottom lip, which was chapped underneath her carefully applied gloss. "The reason you came here is because you were trying to figure out the perimeters of your own magic. You thought these vials would be labeled with a specific power, and that information would help you, which would help Façade."

"No. I came because—"

"You came because you wanted to be a better sub," she said evenly.

Oh. Okay. Meredith had just given me a much-needed alibi. So I wasn't fired; just back to where I was when I'd first found out about this place. "Right. I want to be the best sub I can," I said.

There was a beat, a pause, and in that moment I had to let go of everything I'd just lost. This wasn't the way to crack Façade, but that didn't mean it couldn't be done. It'd only been a few weeks since I'd even learned there was anything wrong. I'd told Vanna to take her time and finish her spy training. Maybe I needed to follow that same advice.

"So. How did you know I was in here? Camera, satellite?"

"Façade doesn't film in the sub-sanitation room. They don't want documentation of what happens in here. But I did see Ferdinand, and knew that if you were wandering around Façade, this is where you'd end up."

"Ferdinand! That reminds me, why didn't you tell me about healing makeup!" My voice echoed against the wall. Okay, so jumping from one hot topic to another wasn't exactly slow-and-steady Desi. But how do these people work here knowing all this stuff?

"It wasn't time for you to know," Meredith said. "That's still in the developing stages, but healing makeup does prove that Façade is thinking about more possibilities than a stand-in for a princess birthday party, doesn't it?"

"Oh. I guess it does."

"See? There're still plenty of wonderful things happening with this agency. And actually, I have some news for you."

My stomach dropped. "I'm not getting sanitized, am I?"

"Of course not. No one knows you're here yet. I only knew because I know *you*. And you have your story in place should anyone watch the security footage and ask questions about why you were roaming all over Façade."

"Okay."

Meredith rolled her eyes. "By the way, it was a royal buzzkill having to rush away from the biggest moment of my life to come find you."

"Sorry about that." I wiped my eyes, trying to remove any trace of crying. "Was your first council meeting good? Are you, uh, happy?"

Meredith flicked my question away with a wave of her hand. "This isn't about happy. The meeting, like I said, was of special concern to you. I have some good and bad news. The good news is the agency has selected your Match."

"Yeah?" I knew this was a distraction, something to make me feel better about my epic magic failure, but I was still biting. I hadn't thought much about my Match. There were only so many possibilities, being as I'd subbed for six princesses, and I definitely had a favorite in that group. If I had to wake up day in and day out as someone else, I would choose Elsa. Not because of Karl, either. Elsa was the princess I identified with the most, the girl I understood. And with understanding came empathy. And with empathy, magic. And with magic, well . . . I didn't know what my magic really meant anymore. "Who is it?"

"Well, Floressa Chase. Of course. She fell in love with you after the secret princess debacle, and is excited to have you at her beck and call. I know how much you love Hollywood—"

"*Old* Hollywood," I said.

"Old, new, whatever." Meredith smoothed out the front of her suit. "You'll not only have a chance to live the royal life, now that Floressa's long-lost father has welcomed her back to Tharma, but the movie premieres and social scene . . . twenty-four-hour glamour. She's quite possibly the most sought-after Match, and she's yours. Or you are hers, I suppose."

"That's . . . great." It was. Really. But the whole glamour aspect of Façade, of life, just wasn't as alluring anymore. The magic, literally, was gone. And Floressa's life might be enviable, but she was also a bit spoiled. Who knew what she would expect of me? And a princess Match could be forever, or at least until I changed departments within Façade. Did I really want to devote the rest of my teen years to Floressa Chase? "What about Elsa?"

"Elsa hasn't applied for a Match." Meredith stood and offered me her hand. "I'd imagine she quite likes her life right now and isn't too keen to escape it. Floressa, on the other hand, has explicitly requested you. A perfect fit."

"When does that all start? The Matching stuff?"

"Soon. You'll receive an entire packet of information on Floressa—far more than what you've previously had available through your manual."

"Oh, so I'll actually know what I'm doing."

"One would hope. Now it's up to you to immerse yourself in Floressa. No more other princesses, no more BEST, no more random jobs. With a position like this, it's expected that Façade time is Floressa time."

I looked around the room, wondering if I would ever see this place again. "So, I probably won't be back at Façade much anymore, huh?"

"No need. You have your own bubble, you have one client. You do have that new substitute ambassadorship that Genevieve discussed, so when it's your turn, you'll come back to address the council as a representative. But you certainly don't need to come back to *this* room in Façade."

Like I could. No way would I make it past security and Meredith a second time. One visit I could blame on curiosity. Another was impossible. "So what's the bad news?" I asked.

"Oh. Nothing devastating. This was bound to happen eventually." Meredith dusted off her suit. "I didn't mention it before your last job because I didn't want you to get dramatic, but the council decided . . . my agenting duties will end. Naturally—I'll be heading a new committee, and I can't be jumping in and out any time one of you girls goes crazy."

I let out a small gasp. "You're not my agent anymore? What am I going to do?"

"The same thing you always do. Get into trouble and cause your higher-up headaches." She smiled weakly. "You'll be assigned someone new, but to be honest, once you're Matched, your agent doesn't have much to do with you anymore. She checks in periodically. In the meantime, Genevieve said she'll take over as a temporary agent, sort of a mentorship until they decide whom to assign you to permanently."

"Wait, why is she doing that?"

"Well, your latest PPR from Vanna was positively glowing—says your magic saved the day. Genevieve is very excited about your future. And I don't need to tell you what an honor that is."

127

"No! Are they trying to punish me?" I stepped away from the vials of magic so I didn't fall into them. All this news was making me feel dizzy. Not only did Genevieve take Meredith away from me, but now she would be watching me all the time. And this was all my doing, because I told Vanna to sing my praises. Stupid! Drawing attention to myself was so not stealth. "Meredith, I can't work here without *you*. This is horrible."

"Oh, hush, I don't much need your diddly twenty percent, thank you."

"But, you're, like, my mentor."

"Mentor? I wouldn't say mentor. . . ." Meredith looked away from me and wiped at her eye. Okay, this was intense. I didn't know the woman even had tear ducts. "This is stupid. I must be allergic to something in this room."

Another wave of tears hit me, and I started to hiccup.

Meredith yanked two tissues out of her purse and handed me one. "I'm sure Genevieve is going to be proud that you figured a way in here, but we're going to need to fill out a report so everything looks legit. Last thing I need is Façade disposing of you because you're too much of a risk. I won't let that happen after all the grief you've put me through. Let's go." Meredith reached over and squeezed my hand, pushing something small, almost lipstick-shaped, into my palm in the process.

Somehow I knew not to mention the object right now— maybe it was a gift and she didn't want me to get sentimental in front of her. I slipped the item into my pocket and followed Meredith into the hallway. My bubble was already waiting outside to take me home.

"So this is it?" I asked.

"Did you want me to sing a good-bye song to make it more official?"

"Can I ask you something?"

"Could I stop you?" Meredith asked.

"Will you let me know what happens with . . . Frank Sinatra?"

Meredith's face clouded. When I'd found Meredith at the Façade Resort, her prince wore Royal Rouge that made him look like the old heartthrob singer and actor, Frank Sinatra. "Frank Sinatra is gone. For good."

"Wait, you mean the real Frank Sinatra, or your—"

"I said no," Meredith said, so softly I hardly heard her. "To the proposal. When you get to this level with the agency, Desi, you can't be anything else. You can't be involved with anyone remotely connected. You know that. Royals, other employees. Off-limits."

"But you love Frank!"

"Of course I love him. I've loved him for many years, and he's one of the only people I've ever loved in my life."

"So you chose this job over love," I said.

"I chose this job over everything. He'll be fine. I'll be fine. It's for the best. Forget my job—he's a royal and I'm . . . I'm just an orphan from Cleveland, Ohio, who happened to have a little magic."

"Meredith, that doesn't matter—"

"Frank and I have no chance of making it with those kinds of odds. We're too different. Even if this wasn't my job, I'm still not in his social class. I'm not from his country. Think of what an awful princess I would make!"

"Technically, marrying a prince doesn't make you a princess, so—"

She held up a hand. "Choosing him would be a massive risk, and if I stay with Façade, I know what to expect, what I can do. I know who I am here." She blew out a breath. "Now, would you please stop making my mascara run, and get in your bubble?"

"Okay—but, Meredith, risks aren't *bad* things. Life is full of risks—"

"And look at what good that idea has done for you. Go. Start preparing for your Match and stay away from this room, got it?"

I wondered when I'd see her again, if we'd ever get another chance to talk. I wanted to do something special, to grasp this moment and make it sharp. Movie lines and favorite quotes scrolled through my mind until I came up with one. "You know what Frank Sinatra said once?" I asked softly. "'I'm gonna live until I die.' You should try it, Meredith."

Maybe what I said was harsh, but no one else was going to tell Meredith that she was making the wrong choice. She looked like she was just about to yell at me again when I slipped into my bubble, the decor of which somehow looked less peppy now.

HOME was already inputted as my destination. Daisy

said to have a safe journey. Whatever. I wanted to go home and stay home. Had anyone ever quit Façade? I mean, voluntarily, without being sanitized? Doubt it. Meredith said it herself—I had the ideal job that most girls would dream of. An uncertain forever of Floressa Chase's shallow life. Glamorous.

I was almost home when I finally remembered the little tube Meredith had stuck in my hand. Maybe it was some makeup that was custom-designed for Floressa so I didn't have to Rouge up all the time.

Not makeup. A small glass tube filled with a blue pulsating liquid labeled CAPRICE.

I let out a squeal. I wanted to rush back to Façade and give Meredith a hug. She might have given up on love, but she hadn't given up on me.

Because Meredith had slipped me her lost sub's magic.

Chapter 14

My bubble bounced into the skating rink party room, and I burst through the entryway. Meredith's faith in me meant I would be able to help a former sub. And if I could help one person, well . . . who knew what could happen after that?

Just a few seconds later, a red and nearly oval-shaped bubble appeared. Reed stepped out, looking like he hadn't slept in weeks. And it very well could have been weeks, the way Façade was able to manipulate time. In Sproutville, it was just seconds later from when we both left, and just a few days since we'd first talked at the cast party.

I opened my mouth before shutting it fast. Reed. What

was I supposed to say to Reed? When we'd said good-bye at Façade, it had been pretty clear he hadn't believed a word I'd said. And yet, now I had proof. Sort of proof.

"How was your job?" I asked.

Reed gave me a weak smile. "Fenmar was brutal. Lots of issues with the government, not to mention family drama. And it's too cold there this time of year."

Fenmar? Wait, FENMAR? *Karl* was the prince of Fenmar. Reed just legitimately confirmed that he was Karl's sub. I mean, I suspected as much, but now I *knew* that my crush on Karl was really a crush on Reed. I liked Reed. Really liked him. My heart did a quick jump, but I pushed back the rising emotions and grabbed the vial. Come on, Desi. Crushes didn't matter when I had the key to magical freedom in my pocket.

"Your ankle is better," he said.

"Yeah, Façade makes a healing powder. Worked like a charm."

"Seriously? Why haven't I heard about that stuff?"

"For the same reason you didn't hear about a lot of things at Façade."

Reed rubbed his eyes. He looked so adorably sleepy, so princely. Agh! My heart kept on hammering.

"I need a nap, but first I have to spray the roller skates." He didn't look at me as he spoke. "Don't feel like you need to stick around for this. Kind of gross."

"It's fine." Yeah, right. He wasn't getting rid of me. I followed him into the skate rental room, which smelled like old socks and lemons. Reed got to work spraying the skates with an antifungal solution, his nose scrunched up with disgust.

I sat down on the bench and watched. Meredith just proved to me that she wanted me to do what she couldn't—to return the magic to Caprice. In Hollywood. I had my own bubble; now I just needed a sidekick. Hey—cool. Sidekick. I could make Reed a spandex superhero suit, and we could call ourselves the Magical Marvels and wear masks so no one at Façade would know who was behind the courageous acts of defiance—

"You okay?" Reed's gentle voice pulled me from my plotting. His ears were red, his attention still focused on the skates. "You seem, uh, intense."

"Huh?" I pictured Reed in his costume for a second and felt myself blush. "Oh. Hey. Just thinking."

"About what?"

"If I tell you, you can't get mad."

Reed rolled a skate along the counter. "I'm never mad at you."

"I just learned more stuff about that story I told you before."

"That was pretty sensational."

"You work for Façade." I shrugged. "You should be used to sensational."

Reed stuck the last skate in a cubby and squirted sanitizer on his palms. He walked around the edge of the counter and held his hand out to me. "Come on. I want to show you something."

The skating rink was still empty as Reed led me to the middle, right under the disco ball. The lights went dark and the ball lit up, the colors dancing to the music that suddenly started. I hoped this wasn't a distraction so he could avoid the topic.

"What's with the special effects?" I asked.

"A distraction."

I knew it. "No, I want to talk about this. Don't think fancy lights—"

"A distraction so any Façade radars think we're being stupid kids and not Enemies of the State."

"Oh. But we're still going to talk."

"Here, dance with me."

He took my hand and touched my waist. Continents could fit between us, but my heart was still doing that million-beats-a-minute thing. "Don't worry. We don't have to be close. Pretend like we're doing something, though."

Oh, I was doing something—something like focusing on the Very Important Mission and not Reed's closeness or his wonderful smell or the whole sidekick-in-spandex idea.

His voice was low when he said, "I thought about what you said the whole time I was on this last job. Every day. Every night."

"And what did you figure out?" I asked.

"Do you know what my talent is, Desi? How I tune into magic?" He stared at me with his trademark I-can-see-into-your-soul stare.

I wiped my hand on my jeans. "Uncomfortableness?"

He pulled me closer. Yes, uncomfortably close. I could

feel his breath on my ear when he whispered, "Truth. I can decipher truth. So I know if someone is making stuff up, or lying, or being evasive, or being honest. It's what makes me such a good actor. And, sometimes, the hardest person to be honest with is yourself. Even for me." He sighed. "If you were telling the truth, then other . . . things were a lie. A big lie."

"Other things" meaning that organic magic—the field his parents had devoted their whole life to—was not the primary fuel of Façade. Or that magic really could be used on non-royals. Or that the makeup and potions could do more than change appearances, like heal a sprained ankle. Or . . . or I didn't even know what else was real or false with our employer.

Reed had that look on his face, like he'd been punched in the gut. I imagined that I looked the same way for a good week after I'd first learned about the sub-sanitation room. Finding out that something you love isn't as pure as you'd thought is like waking up to a magenta sky one day when every other morning it had always been blue.

"Truth. That is a useful talent," I said.

"It's hard, too. I could tell something was off with Façade for a while, but just because I knew there was lie, I didn't know what the lie *was*. I was hoping it was something like, I don't know, the makeup had less glitter than they claimed."

"Ambassador Gregory the makeup pioneer would be so upset."

"Yeah, that would be a small crisis for him."

I pinched my eyebrows together. "But I still don't get why you didn't believe me."

"Because I didn't *want* to. So many people lie, even without meaning to. That's why you always really stuck out to me, even before I found out about Façade. You're an awful liar—you're too good at being good. So, if you tell me that something is wrong, I believe it. I believe you. But I wish you were lying."

"So do I."

The song hit the chorus, and we shuffled in the middle of that floor, the disco ball twirling. Anyone watching would think we were immersed in a romantic moment. Nothing suspicious, except it was sort of dorky that we were here alone. Reed's jaw kept clenching, and he swallowed a couple times, and I couldn't tell if he was holding back anger or tears. Or both.

"So now what do we do?" he asked.

"First, we're going to have to figure out a way to be together more." My ears grew hot. "I mean, so we can talk about stuff without people being suspicious."

"Of course. But that's not what I mean." His voice cracked. "It's just . . . how do we go to work and play the game when we know what we know?"

This time, I was the one who moved closer. I slipped the vial of Caprice's magic into Reed's hand. "Easy. We change the rules of the game."

Chapter
15

Reed and I sent each other fifteen brainstorm texts that night, trying to figure out a place we could hang out without my parents/Façade/Kylee/Celeste and her big mouth getting suspicious. I even considered getting a job at Crystal Palace, a noble sacrifice, considering I couldn't get the foot smell off after two long showers. Reed finally thought of a plan—I could volunteer for the Winter Ball. There was a committee meeting the following week, and Reed already had to work there as part of his job at Crystal Palace. We would have lots of chances to talk, and my parents wouldn't get weird about me hanging out with a boy. Celeste couldn't spread rumors that Reed and I were together, and Kylee—well, Kylee I was still working on.

She didn't talk to me Tuesday at school, despite my attempts to use my magic. I was beyond empathetic, yet I was unable to turn invisible, read her mind, or any other magical miracle I tried to create to force a conversation. When I got Reed alone again, I would have to ask him how he was able to control his magic.

So, that afternoon, I was both nervous and relieved when my phone rang and Kylee's name showed up on the caller ID. As hard as the double-life thing was, having her in my regular life was part of what made my regular life so great.

"You got me pears?" she asked when I picked up the phone.

"I wanted to get a pineapple because they're spiky on the outside but sweet on the inside—kind of like me sometimes. But they were out of season."

"Then what are the pears supposed to say?"

"'Eat me.' The card says everything else." I spent an hour on that card. It's hard to apologize when I couldn't really explain what I was apologizing for. So I'd told her that "Life is black/Life is blue/When it's not colored/With me and you." Okay, so Hallmark said that junk. I just said that she was my best friend, I loved her, and I would never let anything get between us. And I meant it. I didn't know if I could live up to those words, but I meant them. "So do you forgive me?"

"Do you even know what I would be forgiving you for?" she asked.

"For not telling you everything."

"Like?"

"Okay. Fine. You're right." I licked my lips. I couldn't give her everything, but a little truth would help our relationship right now. "I like Reed. Kind of."

"I *knew* it!"

"Well, I didn't. Know I liked him, I mean. And I didn't even know it was him I was liking."

"That makes no sense. Who did you think you were liking?"

The Prince of Fenmar. Duh. "Um, I don't know. It doesn't make sense! I'm an idiot and I'm so sorry and he's totally your crush and I promise I'm not going to do anything about it, because there are far more important things to worry about."

"Like what?"

Shoot. "Hmmm?"

"What's more important than both of us liking Reed?"

"Oh, you know," I said dismissively. "World peace. And our friendship! Besides, Reed and I are just friends. And we're going to stay friends. Besides, hello, you know I'm not even allowed to date yet and—"

"Desi!" Kylee snorted. "Look, I'm not mad at you. I was mad when you were lying, and, yeah, it hurts that you and Reed have this connection. But whatever. You can't control that stuff. I get it. It sucks. But I get it."

There was silence and then a crunch on the other end of the line.

"What was that?" I asked.

"I'm eating a pear. You know they're one of my favorite fruits."

"There were supposed to be grapes in there, too," I said.

"Already ate them."

"So what do we do now?" I asked. "I mean, about Reed?"

I heard her swallow. "I don't know. It's going to be awkward when the three of us hang out."

"It will be because you just said that. Anyway, the three of us never hang out. I'm only going to see Reed now because we're both on the Winter Ball committee—"

"No! What? When did you sign up for that? You can't do the committee."

"Why not?" I asked.

"Because *I'm* doing it. My parents wanted me to get involved with something other than music."

"Oh," I said. "Were you going to tell me?"

"I just did. Were *you* going to tell *me*?"

Silence.

"So looks like the awkward part just started now," Kylee said. I noticed she wasn't crunching on a pear anymore.

Where was the magical button that turned off drama? What if I could hypnotize Kylee with my voice? Make it so soothing that she'd be lulled into a sense of peace and tranquility. So soothing that she'd listen to whatever I said.

I cleared my throat. "It'll be great!" I said, trying to keep my voice balanced between cheerful and crazy. The crazy won out. "Really!"

"Oh, shut up or I'll throw a pear at you. It will be fine. We'll help out, hang out, and make sure nothing is weird. Besides, we might not even see each other."

"Right, you could, uh, help the orchestra with music things—"

"And you and Reed can hang the mistletoe."

"Kylee—"

"I'm kidding. Kind of kidding. Totally kidding." Kylee sighed. "I'm not going to lie. It does hurt. Just don't hide things from me anymore, okay? I'd rather hear about it from you than Celeste Juniper."

"Okay. And like I said, there isn't really anything to hide. And everything is really going to be the same." So much for soothing. How could I make Kylee believe the words when I didn't believe them myself?

That's it. Magic was a waste. I was feeling gallons of empathy, and still nothing. No powers. Just stupid words. "We're not going out, we're just like we used to be, and the three of us can still hang out and it can be totally normal."

Kylee laughed. "Nothing with you is normal. But speaking of abnormal, I saw this movie where these two girls liked the same boy, and one girl was a werewolf, and the other was a dragon, although she didn't know it yet, and it turned out the boy was a killer of, like, magical creatures, so both girls died and he took the head cheerleader to prom."

"That sounds like a stupid movie," I said.

"It actually was. But the boy had his shirt off a lot. I guess hunting magical creatures is great for stomach muscles."

I smiled. Kylee and I were good. Not great, but good. Good would hopefully get us through the next couple of weeks, or months, or however long it was going to take Reed and me to come up with a plan. "And is that story supposed to be foreshadowing for us?"

"No. Unless you're a magical creature and I don't know about it."

Yeah. Well. At least not the creature part.

Chapter
16

I started my Floressa research the next day. Reed and I agreed that we needed to keep working like nothing was wrong. Although I hoped I'd have a while until my Match started, Façade was notorious for doing what they wanted when they wanted. And with the holidays coming up, my life was going to get busy. I had the rest of the week to research, then the first Winter Ball committee meeting was on Monday, Thanksgiving was right after that, and then December and my birthday and the ball and maybe Reed and I would have time to squeeze in a hostile takeover somewhere in there, too.

I still hadn't received any information from Façade, so I

read loads of Floressa Chase gossip online and bought every Floressa magazine, which was nearly half of the grocery store aisle. My dad asked when I had become so interested in celebrities, and I just told him I was comparing old Hollywood with new Hollywood, which seemed to make sense to him. Although I don't know how it could—old Hollywood was the GOLDEN AGE.

Here was the hot buzz around Floressa: she was the long-lost daughter of King Aung of Tharma, which made Floressa a princess. Floressa's actress mother, Gina, had secretly married the king some eighteen years earlier, before a political upheaval led her to leave him for Hollywood. At first, the king reacted badly to the news that Floressa was his daughter, but now there were rumors of reconciliation, that he'd been seen with Gina in random places all over the country. I didn't know if any of that was true, but I hoped for Floressa's sake that the king was at least talking to her. He had another daughter named Isla who was also a big fan of Floressa. Maybe some weird, new family dynamic was being worked out.

My insider information finally came on Saturday morning when a box was dropped off at my house. Make that boxes. Make that moving truck.

There were eight boxes in all. The UPS guy had to use a dolly, and he nearly slipped on a patch of ice on our driveway. My mom stood there in her purple satin jammies, her frown growing deeper with each package. Meredith must have forgotten what it was like to have a real life with a real family and really curious parents; otherwise, she would have never sent the boxes like this. Didn't they have delivery bubbles?

Then I remembered. Meredith wasn't my agent anymore, and Genevieve was taking care of this kind of business now. If anyone knew how important it was to be secretive, it was the head of Façade, and yet here she was sending me stuff through regular mail. The only other explanation I could come up with was that Floressa had sent this herself—but how would she have gotten my address?

I signed for the boxes, noting MIRAGE INCORPORATED on the return address. Mirage was a modeling agency that also served as Façade's cover. So this was from Genevieve. Maybe she was so busy that she didn't have time to think of a more secretive way to ship.

"What is all of this stuff?" Mom asked.

"T-shirts."

"How could you afford eight boxes of T-shirts?"

I hefted the third box into the front entryway. I hardly got it off the ground. "There was a special. And I told you and Dad—my business is doing really well."

"There are stores on Main Street that don't get shipments like this." Mom ran her fingers over the shipping label. "What is Mirage Incorporated?"

"They're, uh, like a clothing company." I gave up on carrying the boxes and started kicking one down the hallway to my bedroom.

Mom shuffled behind me. "Well, can you make me a shirt?"

"Sure." I wiped the sweat off my forehead. This wasn't just files or pictures. Floressa must own a brick company. "Well, I better get working. I think I hear Gracie crying in her crib."

"Your dad took her out for doughnuts. I want to see what's in the box."

"I told you, T-shirts."

"T-shirts don't make a two-hundred-fifty-pound UPS guy grunt when he's picking them up."

"Mom."

"I'm serious, Desi. You're father told me he was worried about you, and I told him you were fine. Was I wrong?"

"No! Are you joking? What kind of trouble could I be in? I live in Sproutville, Idaho. The wildest thing I do is put snarky comments on T-shirts. Oh, and I'm volunteering for the Winter Ball. Better call the cops now."

Mom marched over to my desk and grabbed a pair of scissors. "Then open the box."

I silently cursed Genevieve or whoever had sent me these boxes. Just because they stuck Mirage instead of Façade on the return address didn't make the shipment any less suspicious. Of course my mom was going to ask questions. And I had no idea what was in there. I would think that most of the information—files and pictures and videos—would be uploaded onto the manual. So what Floressa details were inside these boxes?

I went with the lightest box, figuring it was less likely to hold secret-revealing books or files. I tried to block my mom so I could pull back the cardboard flap and sneak a peek first, but she pushed me aside. She kneeled down in front of the box and pulled out . . . a T-shirt.

I let out a sigh of relief. "See?"

Mom held the shirt up, purple with a funky octopus design. "Why would you order shirts that already have pictures on them if you're using them for graphic design?"

I grabbed the shirt and pointed to the back. "Because I'm putting numbers and team names on them. This one is for Team Octopus. It's this game they're doing for the Winter Ball."

Mom pulled another shirt out of the box. This one was a black lacy blouse with little golden buttons down the front. Adorable, but there wasn't an inch of space to print anything. "And what were you going to print on this?" She checked the label. "Desi, this is a Floressa Chase design. Her shirts cost hundreds of dollars." Her eyes widened as she took in all the boxes. "Do you have an online shopping addiction? How much money did you spend?"

"They're all knockoffs," I said. "Not that much."

"Where are you getting the money to buy all of this?"

"I have a job. I'm fine."

"I find it hard to believe that you make enough money designing T-shirts to buy eight boxes of . . . whatever you bought. I'm opening the next box."

Mom sliced through the packaging tape before I could stop her. This box held roller skates and a huge makeup case filled with Floressa Chase cosmetics. Mom pawed through the lotions and perfumes, her eyes getting wider and wider. I wanted to cry. Of all the secrets I'd kept while working for Façade, I was not going to let a UPS delivery expose me. "Why don't you trust me?" I asked.

"I never said that." She checked the price tag on the roller skates. "These are three-hundred-dollar skates."

I let one tear slip down my cheek. "I'm almost fourteen years old and I run my own business. I save for college, just like you guys say, even if college is over four years away. You've never put rules on how I spend the rest of my money, so I don't see how I've done anything wrong."

"Honey, I just don't understand why you're spending money on all this Floressa Chase stuff." Her gaze flicked to my desk. "And all those magazines. They're all about her, too. This doesn't seem healthy. She's not a good role model, and besides, this is expensive and—"

Then I had an idea. A brilliant idea, at least given the amount of time I had to get out of this situation. "Okay. I didn't want to tell you this, because I didn't want you to make a big deal. But the truth is . . . Floressa Chase is my client."

"What?"

"I design T-shirts for her line. And instead of paying me, she sends me stuff. Looks like she went overboard, but you know celebrities."

"So now you're friends with Floressa Chase?" Mom asked.

"I didn't say that. She found me. Online somehow. She

likes discovering really obscure talent, and you can't get more obscure than me."

Mom stared at me. I stared back, my spy training again super helpful. I made sure I didn't blink or fidget or display any other quirk that would indicate dishonesty. Although, I wasn't *totally* lying. I was telling the truth and allowing my mom to believe what she wanted. That should count for something, right? It's not like Façade was giving me many options here anyway.

"Why didn't you tell me about this?" she finally asked.

"I didn't know if it was going to pan out. I sure didn't think she'd send me eight boxes." I tossed the black lace top to my mom. "This is more you than me. You want it?"

I scooted on my knees over to another box and opened it. I kept my expression as neutral as I could. My mom stood, looking at all the boxes, a mixture of confusion and relief on her face. "So . . . this is all just because you design T-shirts?"

"Uh-huh. If you don't believe me, I'll show you my bank account. I think I have about one hundred and fifty bucks in there now. I've been saving hard." No need to mention the thousands and thousands of dollars in my special Façade account, or that I had already saved enough to pay for the first three years of college.

Mom held up the black shirt and looked at herself in the mirror. "I've gotten perk packages from pageants before, but nothing like this. If that's the case, then . . . well, I guess this is a good opportunity."

"It's huge. Who knows what kind of word of mouth she

could generate. One mention online and my sales will fly through the roof. Not that I would let this get too big, of course. School and grades and life are much more important." I leaned my elbow against a box as casually as I could manage. "Try that shirt on; I bet it would look cute on you."

Mom sat down on my bed. "Desi, I think I should tell you something else."

"Fine; you can have the octopus shirt, too. Will you please just trust me now?" I felt a pang of guilt that I was asking for trust. This wasn't a secret I would be able to keep forever. What if I got a job with Façade when I grew up? What would I tell my parents I did then? It wasn't fair to either of us to keep this big part of my life hidden. But in this moment, well . . . what could I do?

"I don't want the shirts. I don't think I'll fit into either of them much longer." Mom ran her finger over the stitching in my quilt. "Another thing your dad said you mentioned to him is that you noticed how tired I've been lately?"

I forgot about the boxes, about Floressa, about Façade. This did not sound good. "Yeah?"

"Well, you're right. I have been."

My throat went dry. "Are you sick?"

"No. Well, I am. But good sick." She smiled. "Desi, I'm pregnant."

"You mean . . . *pregnant* pregnant? Like bun in the oven? Seriously? Again?"

Mom laughed. "Fourteen weeks along. We heard the heartbeat last visit—I wanted to tell you, but I *am* older, and

I wanted to make sure everything was okay. I've obviously been sick, and I was worried maybe I was missing some things going on with you because of I've been laid up—"

"You're having another baby," I said. "Gracie is two, and I'm almost fourteen, and you're having a *baby?*"

"Yes. We're surprised too, but excited, of course."

I thumped down next to my mom on the bed. Here I was, trying to change Façade, and my own family was changing right under my nose. I put my hand on my mom's stomach. It was actually a little rounder than usual—how had I not noticed that? How could I miss something so huge? "A baby. Wow . . . Congrats, Mom."

"You're okay with this?"

"Shocked."

"What do you think you'll feel after the shock?"

"I don't know. I probably would have had a hard time a few months ago." Before Façade forced me to grow up. A lot. "Gracie and this baby are going to be so close in age, but . . . I think it's great, Mom. I'm happy for you."

"That means a lot to me, hearing you say that." She gave me a hug, and it felt so good being close to my mother, knowing that she was okay and—wow—pregnant! "No matter what, I care about what is happening in your life, okay? Know that."

"I do."

She surveyed the boxes. "Well, I'll let you go through your goodies. Tell Floressa Chase she needs to do a maternity line next, okay?"

"I have a million T-shirt ideas if she does," I said.

She squeezed my hand and left. The fact that I just got away with the story proved that my mom had something else on her mind. It was an awful lie—why would someone like Floressa Chase do anything nice for a girl in Sproutville? Floressa had a sweet side, but not *that* sweet.

Whoa. They were having a baby. Finding out about the pregnancy should have made me feel included, excited for our family, and it did, but I also felt alone. Alone because I knew what was happening with my parents, but they still didn't have a clue what was actually going on in my life.

I pawed through the rest of the boxes, finally finding a memo on Genevieve's stationery and a handwritten note from Floressa.

To: Desi Bascomb

From: The office of Genevieve Petrova, Head of Council at Façade Agency

    Please find enclosed information from your Match.

Further packages will be sent as we receive them.

    Regards,

    Dominick

I hadn't met Genevieve's assistant, Dominick, not officially, but I had spoken to him via a video conference call on the manual. He seemed cold but professional, not the kind of guy to mess up something simple like shipping packages.

He had to have been following orders from Genevieve, who needed to find me a *real* agent soon, since the woman was obviously so busy that she didn't think about the consequences of sending Floressa's information directly to my house.

Dear Desi,

Lucky you, right? I thought you'd want a couple of things to help you prepare for our Match. Most of this is last season, so nothing lost. I just want you to get in the habit of wearing my styles, accessorizing with my jewelry line, and moisturizing with my beauty essentials. You'll also find a copy of my scrapbook, which should give you enough history on me. Or you could look online. After all, I was the number-three Internet buzzword last month, right after some war in . . . some country.

And I wanted to, you know, thank you for your help with my mom and my father, King Aung. So this is the ultimate of ultimate down-lows, but things between them are very cozy at the moment—disgustingly so. Like, they're-back-together cozy. Like, they-finish-each-other's-sentences cozy. TELL AND YOU DIE.

So I've also had my people assemble a binder on the king and his country and stuff. We've hung out a couple of times since the news broke about him being my dad. All in secret—it's very new and we don't want the paparazzi watching. He's decent. I'm not going to buy a T-shirt for him that says WORLD'S GREATEST DAD anytime soon, but I like him. Plus, he bought Barrett and me his-and-her motorcycles for our six-month anniversary. They're mint-condition vintage. No touching!

I don't know what happens next. I guess we'll meet up sometime? There is so much about me you still need to learn. Like, did you know my favorite vegetable is broccoli, but only if it's in broccoli cheese soup, and only if the cheese is imported? See? I'm complicated. Get reading.

Floressa

Even though I would have preferred Matching for Elsa, I had to hand it to Floressa—she was very comfortable with who she was. And sometimes, a high-maintenance princess is easier to copy. I could make any demand and it wouldn't be considered out of character. And with Floressa living in Hollywood, it could be fun to ask for all sorts of crazy stuff. Diamonds, expensive cars, lunch with famous actors . . .

Wait. My grip tightened on the expensive tennis racket I'd just dug out of box six. Genius moment. There was one random request I could make, one task that might seem a little weird for Floressa, but still be totally doable. I don't know how I didn't even link the two before. Next time I subbed for Floressa, I could pay a visit to a certain struggling actress who also lived in L.A., an actress who Meredith once knew as a sub—Caprice. I could give her a very special gift.

The gift of magic.

Chapter
17

I'd gone to the Winter Ball every December since I was a baby. I remembered when I was seven, they had a real live reindeer in this makeshift stable across from the community center, and all the kids sat on the fence and watched the animal poop. When I was ten, I earned third place in the city Paint a Winter Wonderland contest, and Celeste was so jealous that she told me only weird people were artists, even though she'd entered a picture too. Sproutville was small, sometimes small-minded, but I always looked forward to the Winter Ball. The buildup to the event was bigger this year, now that I knew how much work went into planning it. The meeting had items of business on everything from menus to entertainment. Reed, Kylee, and I sat in our cold foldout chairs, staring at the snow outside of the community center, while two PTA moms argued over the ball DJ.

Mrs. Gunther, the mayor's wife and Winter Ball chairperson, finally stood and clapped her hands together, blue veins marbling her translucent white skin. I knew Kylee was going to call her a ghost, probably from a movie called *The Mayor's Wife Returns*. "Ladies. We can continue the eighties love songs versus modern-country-music debate at a later time. I appreciate both of your remarks."

The two women mumbled apologies and sat down on opposite sides of the community gym. Reed caught my eye and mouthed, "Save me."

Just when it seemed things couldn't get any more awesome, Celeste Juniper bumped through the doors of the community center with another girl, Annie. Annie used to be my friend in elementary school, but she ultimately sided with Celeste. Although I was over the whole split, I didn't need that tension here when things were already so awkward with Kylee and Reed. There were only so many fruit baskets I could send until Kylee was done with me.

"Sorry we're late! I'm here to get some hours logged." Celeste flipped her highlighted curls. "Part of being a pageant princess is helping out in the community, you know."

"How wonderful," Mrs. Gunther said. "Why don't you have a seat next to the other youth volunteers—we were just about to assign committees."

The girls sat in the row behind us. Annie gave me a

little wave and smiled at Kylee. "Hey, I think you're in my math class."

"Yeah," Kylee said. "That test today was so hard, huh?"

Annie's eyes widened. "I know! When are we ever going to use a quadratic equation?"

Celeste leaned in between Reed and me. "Well, look. It's the happy couple."

"Hey, Celeste," Reed said. "Didn't think you would make it."

"Don't call us that," I hissed. Why was she harping on the couple thing? And wait, what did Reed mean about the "making it"? Did he know she was coming? Did they TALK? "Why don't you go volunteer somewhere else?"

"I didn't know I was crashing your duo." She glanced at Kylee. "Oh, never mind. So it's not couple time just yet."

Kylee stared straight ahead, but she obviously heard Celeste's comment. Great, like things weren't hard enough. Why was Celeste here anyway? Didn't she have a tiara to go shine?

"Next item of business," Mrs. Gunther said. "The decorations committee needs more volunteers to help decorate the trees around the outside pavilion. You need a good eye for ornamentation—"

Reed practically shot out of his chair. "Desi and I can do it!"

"How cute," Celeste said.

I tugged on Reed's shirt. "Reed."

"She's really into, uh, aesthetics," he added. "And I've already been doing some decorations for Chuck at the skating rink."

I snuck a look at Kylee. She was biting her lip and staring at the ground. The only thing she asked was to not leave her out. This was exactly what I didn't want to have happen. "And Kylee is really good at, um, decorating, too."

"Sounds like a two-person job to me," Celeste said.

No way. I was not ditching my friend. I stood up and folded my arms across my chest. "With three, two of us could hang things and the other one could step back and say if it's even."

Mrs. Gunther scribbled a note on her clipboard. "That's a very good idea—"

"But Kylee's a musical genius." Reed's eyes were going to pop out if he kept bugging them at me. Why was he acting like this? "So it'd be really helpful for her to work with the DJ."

"But—"

Kylee's face flamed, and she looked down. "No, it's cool, Desi. Reed has a good point."

"I'm not going to leave you," I said.

"This isn't about socialization, anyway." Mrs. Gunther peered over her glasses at me. Man, she was creepy. "We'll have several adults working on decorations as well, but you two can add a little . . . vim and vigor to the team."

Vim and vigor? What the heck did that mean? I shot Reed a desperate look, but he kicked me in the calf.

"We need to be alone, remember?" he whispered loudly. Celeste beamed. Kylee looked close to tears.

And although I understood what he was saying—that we needed to be alone so we could discuss Façade—I knew how much this was hurting Kylee. But what could I do? This was the only opportunity that Reed and I had a decent alibi to be alone together to talk—this was, after all, the reason we were even volunteering. Decorating the trees would be perfect. We could mute our conversation and pretend to work while we planned. And the things we discussed could help us figure out something bigger than a friendship, bigger than Sproutville, bigger than almost anything.

But if I didn't stand up for Kylee right now, then that crack between us was going to become a canyon. If the tables were turned, this wouldn't have even been an issue, because she would have marched over to the clipboard and signed us all up for the same thing.

Who'd have thought the Sproutville Winter Ball Planning Committee could be so life-changing? "Can we, uh, switch positions? Soon? Can Kylee help with music, but then come help Reed and me later? The music won't take as long. And we do need her help."

"If I say yes, will you kids stop playing tug-of-war?" Mrs. Gunther asked.

"Yes," we all mumbled.

Mrs. Gunther pointed to the gym door with her pencil. "Then, you two, go to the storage closet and start unpacking some of the older decorations. Figure out what is salvageable. And music girl. You come with me. As for pageant girl and your friend . . . you can be on cleanup."

"Clean?" Celeste squeaked. "You want me to *clean*?"

Reed walked away without a look back. The tug-of-war wasn't over for me, though. For the first time, it felt like I had to choose one life over the other, and I wasn't sure if I wanted to follow Reed.

Kylee flashed a false smile. "It's okay. Go."

"No. This is stupid. Just come with us." I grabbed her hand. "You don't want to go sit with some cheesy Sproutville DJ and go through his old CD collection."

"You're right. I don't." Kylee pulled away. "But it'll probably be easier than going with you and Reed. He obviously wants to be alone with you."

"Not because he likes me!" I nearly shouted, frustrated. "Because . . . ugh, because . . ."

"Uh-huh." Kylee shook her head. "I'm going to go."

She joined Mrs. Gunther on the stage.

Why couldn't I help her? Why couldn't I be a better friend? Why did this situation have to be so messed up?

I felt a tingle in my toes and nearly jumped in excitement. There it was. Magic. I didn't know why it came so strongly, probably because my empathy was so intense at the moment. Also, it seemed the more I used my magic, the more naturally it came. Now I just had to channel that ability into . . . something. I looked around the room, but all I saw was a broom. This wasn't the movie *Fantasia*, and I wasn't Mickey Mouse.

"Something else, Desi?" Mrs. Gunter asked. Kylee looked up.

We made eye contact, and I put all my emotion, all my feelings and apology and helplessness into that look. I must have looked crazy, because Kylee stepped back like she'd been pushed. I visualized her mood softening, like a nice fluffy coat or a bucket of kittens. Soft kittens, naturally, without any claws. When she finally regained her balance, her expression went from sad to serene. "It's okay," she mouthed.

It was the best okay ever. I didn't understand how I'd actually accomplished what I wanted to, but I did. My whole body was pulsing, and the warmth felt so good. Annie bumped Kylee's hip, and they started to look at Annie's iPod. Perfect—Kylee wouldn't be alone. And Annie really was sweet, despite her Celeste association. Maybe we could all be friends. Content that Kylee would be fine for now, I turned to follow Reed. Instead, I was suddenly up close and personal with Celeste.

She smiled at me—a genuine smile, or as genuine as Celeste ever got. "Don't worry about Kylee. She'll get over it. That's what good friends do—forgive and forget. Go see your boy."

"He's not my boy," I said, exasperated. "And don't talk to me about being a good friend."

"If he's not your boy, then why did he ask me to volunteer so Kylee wouldn't be the only other girl here?" Celeste poked my arm. "He said he wanted a chance to work *alone* with you. I know you don't have much dating experience, Desi, but trust me. That's code for a boy liking you."

I shook my head. Was Celeste Juniper seriously giving me love advice? "Reed asked you to come?"

"Duh, that's what I said. You're welcome, by the way."

"So . . . so you're being nice? To me?" I asked.

"Look, I owe you after the Miss Teen Dream pageant." She narrowed her eyes. "Not that I wouldn't have placed on my own."

"Of course."

"It's so smart that Reed and you signed up for something that your parents won't care about. Hayden's mom has been so strict lately—I hardly ever get to see him."

This was weird. Girl talk with Celeste. Make it stop. "Oh."

"So, anyway. I totally get it. Annie and I are going to volunteer, we'll hang out with Kylee so she's not lonely while her best friend steals her crush—"

"Celeste!"

"What? I didn't say that boy-stealing is a *bad* thing."

"Of course you don't think it is," I said.

"Desi. You can't sacrifice your own romantic happiness just because someone else might get hurt."

Wow. As tactless as Celeste was, she kind of made sense. And bottom line, this wasn't about Reed and me liking each other. We had to be together for much bigger reasons right now. I almost stopped the conversation there, but then I thought . . . "Hey. I don't like Hayden anymore."

"Uh, yeah. You like Reed. And Reed is hot. So get out

there and make it work. I'll be so mad if you chicken out after all the effort I put into this. I could have volunteered for Hayden's soccer team instead."

"Um . . . okay? Thank you, I think."

"Kylee!" Celeste called. "That music better have a beat to it. We want to dance."

I wandered into the hallway, a little dazed by my Celeste encounter. Had that magic I'd tried to use on Kylee—and I was pretty sure had miraculously worked, finally—somehow bounced onto Celeste, causing her to be, dare I say, *kind*? Was that what just happened? Had my ex–best friend really come to distract my *new* best friend so I could be alone with the boy we both liked? Even stranger, I think the boy we both liked had *arranged* the whole thing, not because he liked me, but because we needed to, um, save the world. Yeah, that's about where things stood. This was totally going as planned. Completely.

When I got to the storage unit, Reed was already hauling out bins.

"Thanks a lot," I said.

"Sorry. Did you want to carry this bin?" He pushed a bin into the hallway. He popped open the lid and yanked out a large strand of garland. "What do we do with this stuff? Disperse the plastic needles?"

"Did you just say disperse?"

"So?"

"It's not a word guys I know would normally say."

"The guys you know must be idiots, then, and it's no

secret that I'm far from normal. You have your manual on you?" he asked.

I readjusted the strap of my purse. "Always."

"So, let's get to work."

I stuck my hand on my hip. "Before we start on that, I have to say that I am not cool with how you ditched Kylee. And what's with you getting Celeste in on this?"

"I had to." Reed frowned. "We can't plan our grand scheme with Kylee around. Being alone to talk is the whole reason we signed up to do this committee. Celeste is just backup. She already started those rumors, so I used her meddling to our advantage."

"So you want people to think we're together?" I asked.

"What does that matter? We have more important things to worry about than junior-high gossip. And is that really such an awful rumor anyway?"

My cheeks burned. "No . . . I mean, yes. Or no . . . It's just, Celeste is not a person I want to feel indebted to, and you could have been a little more sensitive about Kylee's feelings."

"Kylee doesn't care. She likes music."

"That's not the point." I threw a piece of garland at him.

He flopped down, stunned. "What was that for?"

"Kylee likes music, but she also likes *you*," I yelled. "So how do you think she feels when her best friend and her crush are practically running away from her?"

"Kylee likes me?" Reed asked. "No, she doesn't. She doesn't even talk to me."

"Because she likes you!" I threw up my hands. "Are you sure that *truth* is your skill? Because you're kind of sucking at it right now."

Reed fiddled with the fake garland. "It's not an exact science."

"Well, what are you going to do about it?" I asked.

Reed stood and slipped into the storage closet. When he didn't return, didn't rush over to apologize to me or even go back and talk to Kylee, I stormed after him. He was back to rearranging bins, like nothing had happened.

The shot of adrenaline from my Kylee moment was turning into anger toward Reed. I mean, I totally understood his motivations with Celeste, and maybe even his clueless-ness with Kylee. But why the mixed signals? First, he's flirting with me, then he doesn't trust me, then he's all business about our alliance, then he makes these cryptic comments and . . . ugh! You know what else? He should know how hard it was to keep everything a secret. Except, never mind, *his* whole family worked for Façade.

"That's it!" I yelled. "I'm done with this stupid living-two-lives stuff. You and I are going right back into the gym to tell Kylee the—"

"Truth?" Reed snorted. "That'll go over well."

"Do you know what it's like lying to my best friend?" I asked.

Reed dropped the box he was holding and took a step closer to me. And another step. The storage closet wasn't very big to begin with, so now we were almost nose to nose.

I could smell his Reedness, feel his closeness, could see the skepticism in his eyes.

"You think I don't know? My whole life has been about Façade. My whole life *is* a façade. We've moved around so much, I've never been able to make close friends. And if I do, I can't keep them, because part of feeling truth like I do means I know when they start to think I'm weird. So I can't open up. I've probably told you more than I've ever told anyone besides my parents, and that's only because I know you understand what it's like. But maybe you don't."

"I do," I whispered.

"So you get that we might lose more than one friendship here, right?"

I looked away. "Yeah."

"And you're still in? Because I'm not going to go up against Façade unless you're a hundred percent about this."

I cut him a look. "I'm in. But you can still be nice to Kylee."

"I'll save her a dance at the ball."

"Not funny."

"Two dances then."

I couldn't help it. I smiled. And I hated him for it. And loved him. And . . . ugh, WHY WERE BOYS SO COMPLICATED? "You're impossible sometimes."

"Most of the time. That probably doesn't win me many friends, either. But I promise I'll be more sensitive to Kylee. And I'm sorry about Celeste—I didn't know that would be a big deal."

"It's not." I sighed. "And I'm sorry too. I just . . . There's a lot of stuff going on at the same time."

"Is it too much? Do you think you're ready to find this sub?"

I lifted my chin. "It was my idea, wasn't it?"

"Good. Then let's get to business." Reed bent over and hefted a box into my arms. He pushed the door open with his foot, and I followed him into the hall. It took some self-control, but I didn't peek in on Kylee as we walked down the corridor and out the back exit. Cold air blasted through my thin sweater. Reed propped the door open with a rock.

"So, what do we need to do first?" Reed asked. "I mean, you have this vial of magic, but who does it belong to and how are we going to get it back to them without being caught?"

I told him about my conversation with Meredith, about Meredith's sub, about the box of stuff I got from Floressa, and the close call with my mom. And then the good part—that Floressa lived in Hollywood, just like Caprice, so we had a perfect cover plan. Well, as perfect as we were going to get.

"Wait, Floressa Chase is your Match?" Reed asked, his voice cracking with excitement.

I plopped the box down next to the front entrance and crossed my arms over my chest. "Yes, she is, and no, I'm not going to introduce you. I don't care how pretty she is."

"I don't think she's that pretty. She's too done up. And I've already seen her a million times."

"On TV?"

Reed knocked on my head. "In person. I'm Barrett's Match. Prince of Fenmar? Floressa's boyfriend?"

A knot formed in the pit of my stomach. Oh. Barrett. The *other* Prince of Fenmar. So if Reed was Barrett's Match—the idiotic, self-absorbed brother—then he wasn't Karl's Match. Which meant Reed was not the boy I fell for when I subbed for Elsa.

"I thought you were *Karl's* Match," I said.

Reed looked thoughtful. "I don't think he has a Match. I could ask him. But that doesn't really matter now, does it?"

Right. It didn't matter. So Reed wasn't Karl. So what. So Karl . . . really was Karl? Did I feel a connection to Karl when I subbed for Elsa? If so, why did things feel so different between us later? And if Reed wasn't Karl's sub, did that mean I'd based my feelings for him on something that wasn't real? Here I thought I liked Reed for this special reason, when that reason never existed. Great, now I like *two* boys. I think?

I shook my head. So what. SO WHAT, DESI. Crush crises were nothing next to impending magical chaos. I had to do what Reed was obviously doing and focus on the task at hand. This wasn't about us.

But later, when this was all over, that boy and I had some *serious* talking to do.

We headed back down the hallway and retrieved more boxes. It took me that long to find my voice again. "So . . . this is good?" I asked.

Reed scrunched up his face. "Isn't it? Barrett and Floressa

are bound to line up subs so they can go to the Façade Resort together. And when they do, we'll go to Hollywood and talk to this old sub Caprice together."

I was really trying to ignore the twist of disappointment in my stomach. It was better that Reed was Barrett's sub, really. This was the perfect opportunity. What I didn't understand was how Karl could be so inconsistent—he really seemed like a different person when I met him as Floressa's sub. Crud, what if there was *another* sub and I liked three guys? This was like musical chairs of the heart.

But, so what? Does. Not. Matter. Business before boys. "But the chances are good that Floressa and Barrett will leave together anyway, right? I don't see her leaving Barrett alone with her sub if she can avoid it."

"Hopefully, yeah. But Façade might not be too keen on sending two real-life friends out at the same time. And if they do, they'll be watching us."

"Maybe we can figure out how to jam the system? It went down during a big wedding, right before I faced the Court of Royal Appeals."

Reed grabbed the last box, and we walked outside. "I would think that Central Command is even more tuned in to possible bugs after that crash."

"You're right." I rubbed my forehead. I was starting to get a headache, and I couldn't say if it was from the strategizing or Reed-isn't-Karl news.

"Either way, we don't need much time really, just enough to see if this sub—"

"Caprice,"

"Right, see if Caprice remembers anything about Façade. Then give her back that vial and see what happens when she's magical again. And face the consequences, I guess."

"Oh. Is that all?" I asked.

He plopped down the last of the boxes and started going through the contents. He found a yellowed stuffed snowman and laughed. "This thing is hideous."

"Reed. We're talking about doing something impossible."

"Pretty much." Despite his words, his tone was jovial. "We have no idea how the science works. We don't know if Caprice drinks that liquid or breaks the vial or what. We do this wrong, and we could do more bad than good."

He punched the snowman and tried to fluff up the stuffing inside. I grabbed the weathered decoration and shoved it into the bin. "But we have to do this, Reed. You get that? We have to try. Even if we fail. You said yourself—we can't know what we know and do nothing."

Reed's eyes glinted. "Now, that's more like it. I never said I didn't want to do it. The challenge almost makes this fun. Like James Bond."

"We're a long way from fun, 007."

We went silent as we unloaded the rest of the bin. I stacked the ornaments and lights in one pile, random decorations in another. I wondered what kind of budget we would have—at least a third of the ornaments were falling apart. Maybe I could buy a few at the dollar store. My life felt like it was unraveling, but at least I could Christmas up this ball.

I started to untangle a mess of lights, but looked up when I heard Reed laughing.

"What?" I asked. "These lights are hard. Whoever was on cleanup last year was in a hurry."

"It's not that." He shook his head. "I was just thinking . . . when I pulled you out of that dunk tank last summer, I had no idea what I was getting into. Just saw this cute girl who'd gotten dunked by some jerk, and my instincts kicked in."

Cute girl. He said cute. I was very intent on staying professional, but . . . he did say cute. Just pointing that out.

"Now, here we are untangling Christmas lights while we figure out a way to take down our employer. And my parents' employer." He closed his eyes. "Man, my parents are going to go nuts when they find out about what we're doing."

"Are you going to tell them?"

"I don't know. I don't think we can, can we?"

"Maybe just a bit? We should probably learn as much as we can about organic magic before we try to give Caprice back that vial."

"Good point. I'll think about it. There's no rush, really. We're going to have to look at every possible hole in the plan. And we have to swing it so we're both in California at the same time. It could be months before we can act."

"Don't worry. We'll be ready," I said.

We weren't.

Chapter 18

I took the rest of the week off work for Thanksgiving. Not that I had much of a choice—my Granny came up from Salt Lake on Tuesday night and immediately took over the kitchen, insisting that my pregnant mom rest or else "her ankles were going to swell into tree trunks, just like they did last time." I had to do all the dumb chores, like coring apples for the pie and peeling potatoes. Luckily, it seemed Façade was taking a break too, because I didn't get any messages telling me to get to work. Actually, I hadn't heard anything from Façade, except for the stuff I'd received from Floressa. It would be nice for Genevieve to send me an e-mail, even a quick hello text. I'd be happy with an emoticon at this point.

And I missed Meredith. Not Meredith as my agent, but Meredith as my friend. She'd had this huge life change happen, and I was sure that all these big things were going on that I had no clue about. Was she still talking to her prince, even if she'd declined his proposal? Had she been assigned to lead a new agency branch? What did they do to celebrate Thanksgiving at Façade? Wait, it's an American holiday. Maybe they didn't acknowledge Turkey Day at all. The thought of Meredith—who didn't have any family—missing this holiday made me sad. So I slipped into the bathroom and sent her an e-mail.

Hey, Mer,
Was just thinking of you today. I hope everything is going great at Façade. I got a Floressa package from Genevieve delivered to my house, which was kind of weird. Am I getting a new agent anytime soon? Not that I'm complaining, it's just that I miss you. You eating any turkey there today? Did you get assigned to your new branch? Anything else? I'm working on a Winter Ball committee that's pretty fun. Oh, and my mom is pregnant. Crazy, huh? So . . . anyway, just wanted to say hi. Gobble gobble!
Desi

She hated when I called her Mer. Maybe she would write back faster to scold me. I even missed her scolding.

"Desi?" Granny knocked on the door. "What happened to you?"

175

"I'm in the bathroom. Do you need specifics?"

"You have to go to the store. I'm out of butter, and you bought the wrong brand of stuffing."

I unlocked the door and stuck my head out. "It's Thanksgiving. The store won't be open."

"Walmart is open all day. I checked in the newspaper."

Basically, every time Granny came to visit, I became her slave, just because I was older. I mean, if my parents had had kids closer in age, then we could have shared the load. Now my mom had to rest, and my dad had to play with Gracie, and I had to do everything. And this was supposed to be my week *off* of work. "I'm morally opposed to shopping at Walmart."

"Jason!" Granny called.

Dad skirted around the corner. "Yeah, Mom?"

"Your daughter is taking a moral stand in order to get out of chores."

"It's not about getting out of chores."

"You better go, Desi." Dad jingled his keys. "I'll take you."

"If you have the time to take me, then you could just go to Walmart by yourself," I reasoned.

"I think she needs to go just to learn some respect and responsibility." Granny sniffed. "Kids today have it so easy— no responsibility whatsoever."

Despite what Granny thought, I had enough respect to not roll my eyes. And responsibility? I HAD RESPONSI-BILITY COMING OUT OF MY EARS.

"Des." Dad put his arm around me. "Let's just run there together. We'll be back in fifteen minutes."

This is how my dad and I found ourselves in the Walmart checkout aisle thirty minutes later, with butter, stuffing, and a twelve-pack of ginger ale for Mom—who was either sick from being pregnant or from her mother-in-law's extended stay.

"Hey, look." Dad pointed at another checkout aisle. "You're not the only one forced to enter Walmart. Isn't that the boy who saved you from the dunk tank?"

I pulled Dad's arm down. "Don't point!"

"But isn't it?"

I snuck a glance at Reed, who was not alone. His agent, Sergei, was with him, along with two adults I assumed to be his parents. His mom had silky black hair and Reed's same olive skin, while his dad was stout with freckles and a baseball cap. Reed saw me and waved. I looked away. Five Façade employees and one ignorant dad were *not* a good combination.

"Oh, yeah, it is Reed," I said. "Well, we better hurry back so Granny doesn't get mad. I have to chop the onions for the stuffing, you know."

Dad paid for our food and put the bags in the cart. "We have to say hi. I never thanked him for helping you, and he did so well in that play."

"Dad, NO." I tried but failed to keep the panic out of my voice. "It's Thanksgiving. I'm sure they have to get back . . ."

Dad was already in Reed's aisle. "Hello!" He stuck out his free hand to Reed. "I'm Mr. Bascomb, Desi's dad. I've wanted to thank you for some time for helping save my daughter."

"Oh, no problem. And it's good to meet you, Mr. Bascomb." Reed gave Dad a firm handshake. "These are my parents, Christopher and Hera, and this is Sergei . . . uh, Uncle Sergei."

"Desi!" Reed's mom scooted around her cart and gave me a big hug. Her accent was much thicker than Reed's. "Oh, honey. I've been wanting to meet you forever! Things were so hectic during that play, and now Reed has been keeping you all to himself with this Winter Ball work. There are so many things for us to talk about, of course. We'd love to have you over for dinner sometime soon." She smiled at my dad. "Your daughter has been so sweet to my son since we moved here. . . . We hop around so much, he doesn't have much opportunity to make friends, but they just have so much in common, and I'm so glad they're spending time together!"

I didn't look at my dad. I hadn't mentioned that Reed was on the Winter Ball committee, or even that I'd ever spent time with him. I hadn't mentioned Reed *ever*, actually.

Dad cleared his throat. "That's Desi. Friendly and full of surprises."

I started to push our cart toward the exit, the Pearsons following right behind.

"Well." Reed's ears were red, probably from his mom's enthusiastic declaration that her son had no friends. "We're just picking up some things to welcome Uncle Sergei. He's never been here for Thanksgiving, so we decided last minute to whip up a feast."

Sure enough, their cart was filled with canned cranberries, pies, frozen potatoes. Nana would cringe at all the store-bought food, but I'd take it over three days of cooking. Sergei patted the smoked turkey breast. "Yes, I want very much to eat of the traditional American food. It is a great treat to visit the land of Idaho."

"Now where did you say you're from?" Dad asked, taking in Sergei's biker appearance. "Sorry, your accent . . . Is it Russian? I thought your family was from New Zealand."

Mr. Pearson jumped in. "Oh, Sergei . . . he's adopted."

"Yes, yes." Sergei nodded eagerly. "Was very old at time. We are, er, multicultural family."

We stopped in front of the automatic doors. The weather was awful outside, a freezing mixture of rain and slush. I turned to my dad and said, "Dad, can you please pull the car around so I don't get wet?"

Dad looked at the Pearsons, then at me. "Suuurrre. Nice to talk, all. We'll have to have you over for dinner sometime. I'd love to hear more about your family."

Once Dad ran outside to load the groceries and get the car, Mrs. Pearson's hand flew to her mouth. "I said something wrong, didn't I? I'm sorry, I was so excited to talk to someone from work, and Sergei is just here visiting for the day—he really does feel like family, but we forget how odd he seems when we take him out."

"I am not odd," Sergei boomed.

"Right, right. You're all-American," Mrs. Pearson said. "And, Desi, I forgot your parents, are, well . . . They don't share our employer."

Meaning: my parents are not magical and have no clue that I am. I watched Dad sprint around the wet cars. "It's okay. They've been suspicious lately, but it's not like they're going to guess the truth."

"Reed tells me you're already Level Three," Mr. Pearson said. "And you're how old?"

"Thirteen. But my birthday is December tenth."

"Very admirable." Mr. Pearson squeezed Reed's shoulder. "You're a good influence for my son."

Reed hid a smile. So, obviously, he had not told his parents how much I'd corrupted their model-employee son with all our planning and scheming.

"Well, since we ran into you, we have some big news that we're grateful for today," Mrs. Pearson said. "Reed said he hadn't told you."

"Told me what?" I asked Reed.

He looked down at the floor. "Mom, I was going to wait until after the holiday."

"Nonsense. She's bound to hear from Meredith anyway."

Reed sighed. "Can I at least mute the conversation so you don't spill too much?"

"Who would you need to block?" Sergei asked. "This is not big secret. And when did you start with the muting? Is this so you and Miss Bascomb can have talk of love—"

"Dude! Sergei!" Reed pushed his agent, but Sergei didn't budge.

"So, what's the news?" I asked Reed's parents, desperate to save us both from scrutiny and embarrassment.

"We've been promoted!" Mr. Pearson said.

I beamed. Even if I wasn't keen on how the agency was being run, the family's enthusiasm was contagious. "Oh, that's fantastic! But what does that have to do with Meredith?"

"Well, she's the one promoting us," Mrs. Pearson said. "Didn't you hear? She's been assigned to Organic Magic. It's temporary, but we do hope she'll be assigned to our division for good. She's very assertive and driven."

"Yeah, that sounds like Meredith," I said. "What's your promotion?"

"We're exploring ways to maximize the power of our magical sources," Mr. Pearson said. "There's essentially a terminal velocity we can achieve when it comes to harvesting our researched organisms, but we're hoping to find ways to break that barrier and either sap more energy from known sources, or discover a source that has unlimited magical matter."

"Oh."

Reed leaned in. "Basically, they're looking for more magic. Dad geeks out when he gets excited."

"And we finally get to search for the Vorvella tree!" Mrs. Pearson gripped her shopping cart. "We've spent years researching the magical folklore, and now we're only months away from finding it ourselves."

My dad pulled his car around to the sliding doors of Walmart. I needed to make a run for it to avoid getting too wet, but first I had to figure out what the Pearsons were talking about. "So you're going to go look for some tree?" I asked. "Like, for vacation?"

"The Vorvella tree is a legend. It's an Egyptian tree, like the tree of life—its sap can produce an infinite amount of magic. Some people believe Façade used to have one that was passed down to each council head. Lots of the company's shared magic supposedly came from this tree, but an enemy of the agency killed it, or so the legend goes."

"Is not legend!" Sergei interrupted. "Vorvella is as real as turkey in my shopping cart."

"No one knows if the Vorvella is real, because no living person has ever seen one," Reed said. "But my parents . . . they're kind of obsessed with it, and so they've always wanted to move to Egypt and discover another Vorvella for Façade."

"And Meredith approved the funding. So it's finally happening!" Mr. Pearson added. "Isn't that wonderful?"

"Yeah." I couldn't conjure any enthusiasm into my voice. Did this mean what I thought it meant? "That's great. Congratulations."

Reed took my hand. "Here, I'll walk you outside."

I tried to pull my hand away, but Reed wouldn't let me.

Mrs. Pearson smiled knowingly. "Good-bye, Desi! Come by for a visit before we move."

"Yeah. I will."

The Pearsons and Sergei waved. Reed and I stepped outside and paused under the awning. My dad motioned for me to hurry.

"So you're moving?" I asked Reed.

"Seems like it. But don't worry, we'll still have time to work on the, uh, special project."

"I'm not worried about the project right now."

I looked down at our hands, still entwined. So did Reed. Behind the glass, his magical parents and his Russian-prince agent were waiting by their Walmart shopping cart. And fifteen feet away, my dad was grooving in the minivan. Reed's mom said we had so much in common, but geography was not going to be one of those things for very long.

"I have to go," I said.

"This sucks." Reed's jaw tightened. "I'm sorry."

"Don't be. It's not your fault." I hurried through the rain and slid into the backseat of the minivan. Reed stayed outside, his hands deep in his pockets, his eyes sad. I know it was melodramatic, but I stuck my hand on the glass as we drove away.

Like always, my dad was very intent on the road, so I quickly slipped my manual out of my purse. Meredith still hadn't written me back. I didn't bother with e-mail this time, just sent a quick text.

DESI: HOW COULD YOU?

She wrote me back right away. As much as I was missing her before, this was not what I wanted to hear.

MEREDITH: TRUST ME. IT'S FOR THE BEST.

What was IT supposed to mean? Promoting Reed's parents so they had to move and Reed and I wouldn't get to see each other anymore? And if she was really thinking about what was "for the best," then maybe she could find me a new agent instead of busy stand-in Genevieve, one who actually cared about her client's feelings. Not that I was going to write Meredith about that. I was never going to write her again, period.

"So, what's the story with Reed?" Dad asked. "Your mother and I had no idea you two were so close. He's a great kid, honey, but you are young and—"

"They're moving again," I said, monotone. "To Egypt."

Dad's voice softened. "I'm sorry, Des."

I watched the rain pound the window. "Yeah. Me too."

Chapter

19

Reed and I didn't have many more chances to discuss his imminent move, or Vorvella trees, or Operation Caprice, or anything to do with Façade. Part of this was because we couldn't ever find time to be alone, but I think another part was we weren't ready to talk. The news was too big. Just when we were starting to get things going, he was leaving. Sometimes it felt like I'd lost him already.

Kylee, Celeste, and Annie were moved over to the decorations committee the week after Thanksgiving. The committee had received an anonymous donation, so they bought hundreds of dollars of additional decorations, making the setup a larger job. I wondered if Meredith donated the money to keep Reed and me apart. She was good at that.

At least my relationship with Kylee was less awkward. Now that word of Reed's upcoming move was out, Kylee's interest seemed to have lessened to the point that she was now able to talk in his presence. When the three, and sometimes five, of us were together, we just chatted about regular things. Celeste dropped pageant news, Kylee compared everything to scary movies, and Reed charmed us all. As for me, I was more quiet than usual. With the news about Egypt and the revelation that Reed was *not* Karl's Match, I didn't know how to act around Reed. Everything felt so doomsday and dramatic and like there was no hope for us or our Great Façade Plan. Which is not the kind of thing you want to hear while hanging garlands, so I just smiled and kept my mouth shut.

After two weeks of hard labor, it was finally December ninth, the night of the Winter Ball, which also happened to be the night before my fourteenth birthday. I liked the idea that I was exiting thirteen in style, thanks largely to the getting-to-know-me gifts from my Match.

Some of the stuff Floressa Chase sent me had no purpose in Sproutville. Like the red leather pants, or the hat made out of ostrich feathers. But in the latest shipment, Floressa had included a champagne-colored cocktail dress with lace overlay and chiffon. The dress was very old-screen-siren, and I couldn't help but feel like Floressa had designed the piece for me. My mom did my hair in soft waves, and I even let her apply a bit of makeup. My dad got teary-eyed when he saw me and insisted on taking a million pictures. I took a couple of photos of my parents, my mom radiant in her new black maternity dress. Then my mom surprised Gracie and me with an early birthday present, new matching gray peacoats. When we walked out the front door, I caught a glimpse of our whole family, and even though I'd always felt like the odd girl out, tonight we looked like we all belonged together.

The transformation of the community center was magnificent, which I had to say was mostly due to Celeste's input. She'd had the idea to string lights into a canopy over the gym with organza underneath, so that it felt like we were in a large white tent, not the place my dad played basketball on Saturday mornings. Then again, she also suggested they replace the Christmas carolers with hip-hop dancers, a request that was not granted.

We got there early, and I went straight to the ice-skating rink, hoping I could steal a few minutes alone with Reed before Kylee got there.

I wrapped my peacoat tight around my middle as I walked outside to the man-made frozen pond. "Have you seen Reed?" I asked his boss.

"The decorations lady had him putting some lights up in the magical forest. If you see him, tell him to hurry back. Skaters are going to be here soon."

Reed was scheduled to sub for Barrett in L.A. sometime this weekend, but Floressa didn't have me down until March. It seemed a little odd that Barrett would want to leave when he was in America visiting his girlfriend, but Reed said Barrett was getting tired of all the drama happening in Floressa's life. Supportive boyfriend he was not, although at least Floressa had no clue that Barrett was peacing out and using a sub.

Reed looked at his job in L.A. as a plus—he'd have a chance to scope out the scene, maybe find some leads on where Caprice lived so that when we did finally sub together, we could contact her quickly. But I didn't like the idea that Reed would be with Floressa. As Floressa's boyfriend. Yeah, yeah, it's part of the job, but would you want the boy-you-think-you-like hanging out with a gorgeous teen celebrity/princess? Exactly.

I slipped into the "magical forest"—a small grove of trees planted before I was born, exclusively for this festival. We decorated a bunch of these trees, but there were also some sponsored by different businesses. I touched ornaments made out of nails and screws, courtesy of a hardware store. Then I heard a beeping in my purse and fumbled through until I found my manual. Reed must be leaving.

But no. An e-mail. And not the apologetic one I'd hope to get from Meredith, who hadn't said boo except for her stupid text about Reed.

Ms. Bascomb:

You've been assigned another substitute position as a special request from Floressa Chase. Since your Match's needs are now yours, you will sub for Princess Elsa while spending time with Floressa Chase, thus giving you the

unique opportunity to acquaint yourself with your Match
while working in the field. You have previously subbed
for Princess Elsa and thus should have some familiarity
concerning her personality and standing. Additional
information will be sent concerning your princess, but
remember the duality in your purpose. Please see that *both*
of your clients' needs are met. Façade is an organization
built upon a rich tradition of impeccable impersonation.

Please employ your personal bubble ASAP.

Regards,

Dominick

Administrative Assistant to Genevieve

What in the world? This is the notice I get? Genevieve
had to have known about this job before now. Reed gets a
schedule; I get a last minute client switch. I didn't know
what Genevieve was thinking—if she was thinking—but
at least she had given me a client I knew. I adored Elsa.
Subbing for her had been pivotal for me as a person and in
my Façade career. But why was I subbing for her *now*? Why
would Floressa want me as Elsa, and not just as Floressa? And
why did Elsa agree to this anyway?

I heard a crunch of pine needles and tried to stuff my
manual into my purse, but I fumbled and it hit the ground
instead. Kylee stepped into the little grove. She wore the
short black dress she usually wore to her clarinet concerts,
with layers and layers of scarves and sweaters over the top.
"Hey, what's that?"

"Nothing."

"Doesn't look like nothing. Show me."

Kylee had found me during a moment of weakness. I seemed to be an afterthought to Genevieve, and my former agent had all but deserted me. If I succeeded the way I hoped to succeed, meaning, if I found Caprice, then I might not even have a job anymore. And I was sick of all the secrets and deception, especially when it came to my best friend.

I held on to my manual, deciding what to say. What if I didn't tell Kylee anything, just showed her? Then I wasn't breaking the rules, right?

"Did you get a new phone?" Kylee had on her rainbow mittens and held a cup of hot chocolate in each hand. "Your mom said you were out here freezing, so I brought you some warmth. Can I see your phone? Here, I'll trade you."

This was perfect. She would click around on the manual, see the application with princess profiles, or some frequently-asked-questions section that would reveal everything, and then she would understand why I'd been so weird and had to spend time with Reed, and everything could just go back to normal. Or a new version of normal.

"Desi?" Reed's voice was just on the other side of the trees. "I need to talk to you. Are you in there?"

I didn't say anything. I let Kylee have my manual, and nursed my hot chocolate while she explored. I raised my drink to my lips and took a sip, the liquid burning my tongue. Kylee's eyebrows were knit in confusion as she clicked around on the manual. "What is this?" she asked. "Some virtual role-playing game? What's with all the princess stuff? Dungeons and Dragons?"

Reed barreled through the trees. "Desi, I got the call. So I'm leaving now, but I have a plan to get you there— Oh." Reed finally noticed Kylee, who wasn't looking at either of us. She was mesmerized by the manual. "Wait, what is she doing?" He stepped closer and snatched the manual out of Kylee's hands.

Kylee blinked at Reed. "Hey! I was looking at that. I can't believe how many application things they have for a virtual game."

The hardness in Reed's face softened. "Cool, huh? Sorry I grabbed it. I'm always asking Desi if I can use it."

"Hey, Truth Boy. No lying." In one fluid motion, I reached around Reed and grabbed his manual from his back pocket. "He doesn't need to borrow mine. He has is own."

Reed stepped toward me. "What are you *doing?*"

I shrugged. Now that I'd had a second to think, I realized how stupid I was being. Reed and I had a major task ahead of us, and the last thing we needed was Façade watching us or punishing me because I blabbed about the agency. Our contracts even said to keep our mouths shut. But if I failed, they were going to take away my magic and memory anyway. Maybe Kylee could remember my magic for me.

Kylee tossed Reed my manual. "Here, take that one. They look expensive. Did you order them online?"

Okay. So unless I outright said, *Kylee, we are both magical royal substitutes and these are our manuals that provide us with information about our royals,* she was never going to guess what was going on. And if she didn't guess, I couldn't tell. I blew on a stray wisp of hair. "Yeah. My dad got it for me. It's, like, a beta model. I don't know if it's out yet."

"Well, I want one. Maybe for Christmas." Kylee glanced at Reed, who was closing his eyes and breathing deeply. "What's with him?" she whispered.

Reed's manual started to buzz in my hand. The words ACTIVATE BUBBLE IMMEDIATELY scrolled across the screen. "Uh . . ."

"Kylee, can you do me a favor?" Reed asked. "I was supposed to put some more candy canes on one of the trees, but I left them inside. Can you go get them?"

"Are you getting rid of me?" Kylee asked, half joking, half not.

"It's freezing out here. I'll come with you," I said. "Just give me a second. Reed was going to show me a new app he downloaded."

"Okay." Kylee shrugged. "Wow, must be fun. I'll have to borrow that again later."

Reed and I waited in frozen anticipation until Kylee finally left. We breathed out at the same time, our sighs hanging in the air.

"What was that all about?" Reed shouted.

I kicked at a tree branch. "I don't know, okay? I had a moment of weakness. She saw my manual and then—"

"You almost told her!"

"So, I'm not perfect!" I set my hot chocolate down on

a nearby bench. "I messed up. We already know I'm not a model employee over here."

"You know if they find out that you told, they'll sanitize you in a blink."

"Yeah, well, there are lots of things they could sanitize me for lately."

"Trade me." Reed handed me my manual. The same message was on my screen. That's right. Now that I had my own bubble, no entrances by Meredith. Or Genevieve or her assistant for that matter. One click and the bubbles were here and we were gone.

"I just got the confirmation from Barrett that he is leaving because he needs a break from Floressa. She's tripping out," Reed said.

"Yeah, finding out your dad is a king who used to be secretly married to your mom would make a girl slightly stressed. Barrett's such a jerk."

"I think he doesn't know how to handle it. Royals don't usually show emotion, you know?" Reed rubbed his bare hands together and blew on them for warmth. "So we go forward with the plan. I'll scope out the scene, see if I can figure out where this sub is, so that next time we go to L.A. as subs together—"

"Good news. I'm subbing too," I said.

"But Floressa wasn't on your schedule."

Our manuals started to flash and beep. They were going to burp out a bubble any minute.

"She wasn't," I said. "She isn't. I'm subbing for Elsa."

"Karl's new girl? Does she even know Floressa?"

I scrunched my nose. "You'd know better than I would."

"Ah, shut up!" Reed yelled at his manual. "We only have about a minute. Listen. This might be the perfect decoy. Think of all the craziness that's going to be happening with the wedding."

"Wedding? Floressa and Barrett are getting *married?*"

"No, Gina Chase and the King of Tharma are getting married in a secret ceremony. Floressa didn't mention that?"

Floressa shared a LOT with me lately. Five more boxes of expensive junk, one box filled with magazine interviews and video clips. And don't get me started on the bogus "meal plan" she was trying to enforce. The root diet—if it wasn't covered in dirt at one time, I couldn't eat it. But something major like a wedding? No. Must have slipped her mind. "She didn't."

"I'd think it'd at least be on her latest Match letter to you. That's how I found out from Barrett."

"I didn't hear from Floressa." Just from Genevieve's assistant, who was very bad at mentioning IMPORTANT DETAILS LIKE ROYAL WEDDINGS.

No wonder Floressa wanted me there as someone else. She probably needed help coping with this huge change and knew I would understand, because I was there when Gina and the king reunited. "I can't believe they're getting married. Last time I was there, he wouldn't even talk to her."

"Hey, you weren't speaking to me a couple of weeks ago,

either." He coughed. "Look, we have to go. We can discuss this more when we get there. I'll feel out the Caprice situation and contact you as soon as I have something." Reed finally pushed a button, and his manual seemed to sigh in relief as his red bubble dripped out.

"But we're not ready for full execution yet!" I stomped my foot in the snow. "I was going to try to research Façade's history some more, see if it said anything about returning stolen magic. And maybe we could get you into Façade somehow, or there are clues at Specter, or—"

"It's not like there's a secret box holding all of Façade's secrets. We'll see if the opportunity is right. If not . . . we try again later. For now, though, we need a code word so we can check that we're talking to each other and not the real royal. What do you want?"

I thought about suggesting, "Here's looking at you kid," from the movie *Casablanca*, because that's what Karl said to me way back when I subbed for Elsa, and it's what Reed said to me right before opening night. It was the expression that made me think Reed was Karl. But no, he was Barrett. Just a coincidence, and not something I cared to bring up again.

"I don't care."

He glanced around at the trees. "How about evergreen?"

"Are you kidding?"

"It's not a word you use every day. You have something better?"

"No. Evergreen. Fine." I couldn't be sure, but the red in Reed's bubble seemed to be getting angrier. I pushed the button on my own manual and my yellow bubble zipped out. "Okay. Let's do this."

"Do you have the vial with you?" he asked.

I held up my clutch. "Always. I keep it with my Rouge and manual."

"Good. We'll figure out how to get to Caprice." Reed lowered his voice. "And can you promise me something else?"

He looked adorable in the dim twilight, his forehead creased in worry and concern. A white dress shirt and tie were just visible under his red parka. I started to feel the bigness of this moment—after he moved, we might only get to see each other when subbing for other people. And under different circumstances, being alone in a grove of trees with twinkling lights . . . it might be romantic. Maybe he felt that too, maybe he was going to ask me to be his girlfriend. An oath to each other before our dangerous voyage. I reminded myself to keep breathing. "Yeah? What is it?"

He took my hand and gazed down at me intently. "If you get back way before me and start doing last-minute decorations, don't go overboard on the tinsel."

Dork. I pushed him into his bubble and laughed at myself. He may be mature for his age, but he's still an oblivious boy.

And my hand still buzzed from his touch.

I had one foot in my bubble when I heard a crack. I whirled around to see Kylee's mouth wide open, a box of candy canes in her hand. She couldn't see the bubble—only those with MP can see the bubble—so I pointed up at a tree and yelled, "Look!"

I would get home less than a second later. So would Reed. We would make up a quick excuse if we were standing somewhere different or looked a little different, and Kylee would believe us, just like she did with the manual, because a logical explanation made much more sense than the truth.

I used her shift in focus to rush inside. But there was this quick second before my view went from the forest to the interior of the bubble that I saw Kylee look back at me. I would have thought she'd just seen me disappear into the air, but a word formed on her lips.

"Bubble."

Chapter 20

"Welcome, Desi. Destination: Hollywood Hills, California. Please make yourself comfortable."

"Thanks, Daisy," I mumbled. I curled up into my swivel chair and tried to ignore the stress headache. There was no way Kylee saw the bubble. No way. Meredith and I once popped into the middle of a busy casino in Las Vegas, and no one even noticed us. And actually, once the bubble came around, I was supposed to be invisible, too. I don't know when the magic officially protected me, but definitely before I stepped inside, otherwise there'd be a floating person disappearing into thin air.

The only way Kylee could have possibly seen me was if

she had MP. The chances of Reed, Kylee, and me all having MP and living in a dinky town like Sproutville was close to impossible. And why wasn't she working for Façade if she was magical?

Unless her MP hadn't been ignited yet. The radar at Central Command only monitored the magic of those who'd had that interaction with a magical organism. And she was perceptive, that's for sure. I mean, my mom believed my Floressa Chase story with all those boxes, yet Kylee always suspected something more was going on.

So . . . what should I do? If Kylee does have magic, do I tell her about it? I kind of have to, right? She was going to ask about that bubble the second I got home—if I even came home in my bubble; who knows what Façade did after subs were sanitized. Which is what I'd wanted, for her to figure things out on her own. I just never imagined she'd discover the truth *because* of her own magic.

"Desi, please make sure your makeup is properly applied to allow time to transform. And thank you for flying with Façade today."

I fumbled through my purse until I found my compact. I tried to keep my hand steady as I swiped a touch on each cheek, pausing after to stare at myself in the mirror. I didn't have time to figure out what had just happened with Kylee, but I would mention the sighting to Reed. Right now, I had a job to get to, a job that—thanks to Genevieve's omissions— I was not nearly as prepared for as I should be.

I scrolled through the usual research channels—the

tabloids, the Façade newsletter. Not even an allusion to a marriage. The tabloids were still debating if the king and Gina were *talking*. This marriage, if it was even happening, had been kept highly under wraps.

"Beginning initial descent," Daisy chirped. I clicked on the sub chat room. I'd spent weeks researching Floressa, and now I had only a couple minutes to look up Elsa. Granted, I'd subbed for her in the past and talked to the real Elsa while subbing for a princess at an art exhibit. Still, she hadn't been in the tabloids as much since the Floressa drama happened, and I had no clue where she presently stood with Karl or within royal circles.

Bingo. I was a little jealous when I saw a recent post from an Elsa sub, but I shook it off. I'd Matched for Floressa. Elsa couldn't have requested me if she'd wanted to.

THECOUNTINGCOUNTESS: Looks like Princess Elsa and Prince Karl are still going strong. While I was subbing for Elsa, I never saw Karl. Elsa is away at finishing school in London now, and Karl obviously had prince duties to do in Fenmar, BUT they e-mail and talk on the phone a lot. Kind of a gooey relationship—hard not to throw up at some of his letters. I was only there for a night for Elsa's calculus test. Fourth test I've taken for a princess this month. If anyone ever says that you won't use advanced math in real life, this just proves that wrong.

The post didn't tell me why Elsa would agree to leave

during what potentially could be the biggest royal event of the year, but then again, maybe she didn't know she was ditching out on the wedding. The important thing I knew was that Karl and Elsa were still together and that Elsa was back in school.

I held on to my armrest as we landed and came to a halt. I stood and my neck creaked. As great as it was having the freedom of my own bubble, I did miss the smoothness of Meredith's ride. But not Meredith, of course. Not only had she literally taken Reed away, but she'd allowed Genevieve to step in as my "mentor." If Meredith was so smart, she could have at least made sure I was in better hands. Power must have changed her. I couldn't believe I'd felt bad for her prince—he was probably much better off without her. I know I was.

Two minutes later, the Rouge kicked in and I was Elsafied, huge eyes, golden hair and all.

"You're here!" Floressa squealed just as soon as I'd stepped out of the bubble and into . . . her bedroom? Or maybe a high school gym decorated like a bedroom, because one person could not possibly have a living space this massive. Floressa was lounging on a purple comforter on top of a canopied bed. The damask wallpaper and funky accents were all cute, but what I didn't get was the wall of pictures, head shots, and magazine clips, all of Floressa. Only Floressa.

She noticed me staring and clapped her hands. "There was this old Oprah episode that said you should do a dream board to inspire you to grow."

"But those are all pictures of you," I said.

"No, duh. That reminds me WHO I AM so that I stay that way. I mean, I'm not going to put an astronaut up there. Why would I want to be anyone else?"

Humble.

She patted her bed. "Come sit by me. We need to dish."

I plopped down on the bed next to Floressa, still awed by the size of the space. Did I mention there was another bed on the other side of the room?

"Why do you have that bed?" I asked.

She frowned. "So I can rotate. It's bad for your back to sleep on the same mattress every night."

"Says who?"

"Experts." She squeezed my arm. "Now, isn't my plan genius?"

Genius was not the first word that came to mind when I thought of Floressa. "What plan is that?" I asked.

"My plan to bring you here, Desi." She covered her mouth. "I mean—oops! Elsa."

"Because of the wedding?"

She tightened her grip on my arm. Ouch—she must have ditched the roller-skating and taken up weight lifting. "WHO TOLD YOU ABOUT THE WEDDING?"

Oops is right. If Barrett left to get away from Floressa, he wouldn't have told her he was gone. And he was probably one of the only people who would know about the wedding. "It was in my sub information," I said. "Sometimes they add more than you do, to help us prepare."

She sat back. "Oh. Good. Because this is the most top

secret event in the history of top secret. The only other person who knows is my little sister, Isla. Half sister. You met her, right?"

"She's cute," I said.

"She's crazy. Totally fan-girls on me all the time. It gets annoying." She braided a piece of her long black hair. "Oh, and I told Barrett, so he'll know to be extra-supportive. And Ryder, but that's a given because he's designing my gown. And now you."

"I'm honored," I said.

"So do you see why you're here? I needed someone to help me through this. If I had you sub for me, then I would miss out on all the partying. This way, it's like you're my lady-in-waiting. And since Elsa is a princess, and now I'm a princess, and we're dating brothers, no one will think it's weird that we're beffies. See? Genius!"

You know what? It kind of was. Floressa was good at figuring out Façade's loopholes. Lady-in-waiting/errand girl was how she viewed my job anyway. This was going to be easier than the last time I subbed for her, that was for sure. Not to mention, Elsa wasn't going to be in the spotlight as much as Floressa, so I might get an opportunity to search for Caprice. Uh, with Floressa's boyfriend. Yeah, that kink was going to need some work. "So what can I help you with, my lady?"

Floressa scrunched up her nose. "Don't do that."

"You said I was your lady-in-waiting. I was being funny."

She sighed. "That's right. I forgot how nerdy you are."

"Hey!"

"That's okay. It's not your fault. You were probably born that way." She rolled off her bed and glided over to the large vanity table. Actually, I think it might have been a kitchen table converted to a vanity table. Nearly ever inch was covered in some sort of makeup or cream or lotion. She opened a glass cube on the corner of the table and removed a bedazzled perfume bottle. "I designed this fragrance myself. It's my trademark scent. I patented it so no one else can wear it."

"It's nice to see you're using your power and influence for good."

She applied another coat of mascara in the mirror. "I'm not paying you to be sarcastic."

"Then what are you paying me for?" I asked. "Should I be fluffing your pillows? I've never done this friend-princess thing."

"Oh, we aren't real friends."

"I know."

"Good. No offense, but I don't want you doing *Behind the Celebrity* on Floressa Chase someday and claiming you know me. This is business. Although I will say you have beautiful hair."

"Um, it's not mine. But I'll let Elsa know."

Floressa tossed her own shiny locks. "So the first thing we need to focus on is my dress. Ryder and I are designing it, but there are still some last-minute tweaks and accessories. Since you *were* me, I figured you'd have good insight on what works." She puckered her lips as she looked at Elsa's clothes—a blue polo shirt with khakis. For how beautiful she was, Elsa's style was still very functional and no-nonsense. "And I'll have Ryder make you something nice to wear, too."

I smoothed down my shirt. I wanted Elsa to look good for Elsa's sake. "I can't believe Elsa would miss this. A royal wedding has to be one of the biggest events since she joined the royal scene. How did you convince her to leave?" I asked.

"Her grouchy grandma—"

"Nana Helga?"

"I don't know. She used to be royal but quit for some reason—"

"That's Nana Helga, then."

"Whatever! Nana Helen—"

"Helga."

"—finally agreed to go on a vacation to the royal resort with Elsa. So they're there together, bonding."

"Nana Helga is really making progress if she is using Façade's services," I said.

"Yeah. I don't care. And Karl went too, so they could have some time away from the press."

"Karl has a sub?" I asked, trying to sound nonchalant. Because if Reed wasn't Karl, then maybe this sub Karl was using was the same sub I'd hung out with last time I subbed for Elsa. I no longer put as much value in that magical day, but it'd be nice to at least know who I had been with. Was it Karl, or an entirely different sub? "Will the real Karl be back at all, or is he gone the whole time with Elsa?"

"Um, this isn't about Elsa or Karl. It's about me."

"Still, it was nice of Elsa to let a random girl come sub

for her just so you could have help."

"I might have told her I'd ruin her reputation if she didn't leave. Just a little extra motivation."

Oh. So that made more sense. "Did you think about what *she* would want?"

Floressa unscrewed her mascara and started to glob another coat onto her lashes. "I didn't pay for a guilt trip, either."

I bit at a nail. As sweet as Elsa was, she wasn't one to back down because of a threat. Seeing her grandma and Karl probably outweighed any appeal of hanging out with Floressa. "So what's the next thing we need to do?"

Floressa set down her mascara and turned to look at me. "The guest list. My mom and Aung are telling everyone that this is a holiday party, and then they're going to surprise them with a wedding. Well, my mom said I could only have two people come, but I was barely able to narrow it down to fifteen. So you need to figure out how to get everyone in."

"*I* need to figure that out? I don't know security or who these people are or—"

"You're magical. You can do it." Floressa walked over to her closet and started digging through dresses. She held a silver flapper-style dress against her chest and scrunched her nose.

"And then what?" I asked.

Floressa threw the dress on the ground and grabbed a black strapless number. "Hmmmm?"

"What's my last item of business?"

"Oh. That's easy." She smiled at me. "I need you to ruin the wedding."

Chapter
21

Floressa twirled in the mirror.

"Wait, did you just ask me to ruin the wedding? Like, your mom's wedding?"

She held out her hand and examined her manicure. "Yep. If my parents get married, it'll mess everything up."

"They're your *parents*. Don't you want them to be together?"

"Hold on. I'm hungry. Let's go have the chef make us something yummy." Floressa yanked me off the bed and thread her arm into mine. She peeked out the door, then pulled me into the sun-drenched hallway. It seemed the entire house was made out of glass. "If my parents get married, then my dad is going to think he can suddenly be my real dad and be all discipliney like he is with Isla. And he wants me to move to Tharma and live in his palace and basically give up my whole life. And my mom is just so stoked to have him back that she doesn't see how this move could ruin her career. Have you ever heard of Grace Kelly?"

Please. "Yeah, she was an actress in the fifties who married the Prince of Monaco—"

"—and then never worked again. Oh, and she died in a car crash, just like Princess Diana. So, hmmm, what would you choose?"

We reached the expansive living room, and Floressa flopped onto the couch and pushed a button on a large remote built into the wall. "Javier, I want a beet salad. And Elsa wants . . . ?"

"A grilled cheese," I said.

"Make that, two beet salads." Floressa shook a finger at me. "You're supposed to be on that root diet I sent you."

"I turn fourteen tomorrow. You shouldn't do a crazy diet like that at fourteen. Or ever."

"You're only fourteen? What are they doing sending me a little kid?"

"I'm only two years younger than you. And this little kid saved your butt back in Tharma."

"You have some spunk." She tapped her chin. "I can't decide if I like that."

I lowered my voice. "So you're really going to destroy your mom's love life because you're worried about her job? She could never work again and be fine, moneywise."

"Oh, not just her job. Mine, too. I don't have an Academy Award to lean on. Do you know how much effort it takes to be famous just for being famous? I have to be at every party, take every opportunity I can. Sure, after the wedding, there'll be some interviews about Princess Floressa, but then that'll get old and I'll be left living on some remote island that doesn't even have a Gucci store. No way."

"But if they're in love and happy—"

She held out a hand. "I don't care. They were both fine before they hooked up again. It's just going to mess up my life. I mean, yes, let them have the party, because that's great press, but then you need to do something really big that's going to end their whole relationship. That night, because then Elsa gets back and she'll go into the let's-use-our-influence-to-save-the-world junk that she and Karl are into. Blah."

Javier came out wearing a white chef's hat. He lifted the domed lid with great ceremony and unveiled our beet salads. Floressa tucked her legs underneath her on the couch and proceeded to inhale her food. The beet juice stained her lips. I stared at her in disgust until she finally paused her shoveling to say, "What?"

I couldn't believe this girl. How could I in good conscience take this job? She wanted me to impact her life at the risk of destroying others. I couldn't do that. I knew her mom, Gina. I liked Gina. When I'd last subbed for Floressa, I'd seen how upset Gina was when she got into a fight with

King Aung, and now they were happy. Floressa's half sister was happy. Why couldn't Floressa just go with it? Not to mention, if anything went wrong, Elsa would be Floressa's scapegoat. Real Elsa, not me. This went against everything I stood for as a sub. I pushed the plate of beets away and stood.

"Sorry, Floressa, but I'm not your girl. I'm not going to help you ruin your mom's wedding."

Floressa's fork froze midway to her mouth. "But you have to. I'm paying you."

"Keep your money."

"But you are the only one who understands what I'm going through."

I patted my pocket for my manual. I would summon my bubble and go tell Meredith, or I guess Genevieve, why I couldn't do this job. I didn't know what happened when you refused to do a gig, but everyone had limits, and Floressa had crossed mine. "You couldn't pay me enough to ruin someone's life."

"I'll pay you double." She set her fork down and kneeled down on the carpet in front of me. "And you're not ruining their life. Just their wedding."

"No." I had no idea what Floressa paid, but I could only guess that I made a lot of dough at Level Three, probably more than my dad made. Still not enough to sell my integrity.

"Triple?"

"Floressa? Where are you?" A voice, a very familiar voice, called from the front entryway.

"It's Bear-Bear." Floressa jumped up and glanced wildly around the room. "Don't tell him about my plan. He'll say it's a bad idea."

"That's because it *is* a bad idea."

Floressa crossed her arms over her chest. "Look, are you going to do this or not? Because if you don't, I'll give you a really bad PPT."

Princess Progress Report. "It's PPR." And what did I care about that? Floressa could say I did the best job ever and it wouldn't erase the trouble I'd get into if I got caught searching for Caprice.

"Whatever. I'll make it so you can't sub anymore."

"Flossie?" Barrett was getting closer.

I let out a frustrated grunt. I didn't care so much about my future with Façade, but I did need to stay on this job. Reed and I were never going to get another opportunity like this. So I looked Floressa straight in the eye and . . . bluffed. "Destroying the wedding would go against, er, royal confidentiality agreements to harm another royal. And there's another rule that says I can't defile Elsa's reputation. The agency won't allow it. If they found out what you're doing, they wouldn't send you another sub. Not ever. You'd lose me as a Match, too."

Floressa's face fell. "Really?"

"Really." I tried to keep the relief out of my voice. "Sorry. But I can totally help you with your dress and getting all your guests into the wedding. And that'll give you time to reconsider doing anything drastic."

"Oh." Floressa blew out an exasperated breath. "Fine. Stay. Stupid agency rules."

"Right." And I *never* break agency rules.

"Guess I'll just have to ruin the wedding myself," she said thoughtfully. "And find a way for you to accidentally help, so I can blame you later. Yeah, that'll work."

"What? No, I won't—"

Barrett came barreling into the room. "There you are!" He rushed over to Floressa and swept her into his arms.

She squealed. "Don't kiss me. I have beet breath."

"I love beets." Barrett leaned in to give Floressa a passionate and uncomfortably long kiss. When they came up for air, he grinned at me and said, "Hey there, Elsa. I could give you a kiss, too. You know, from my brother."

Floressa pinched his arm. "Don't even joke. Besides, if she likes Karl, she obviously wouldn't like you. You're too handsome."

"Smart girl." Barrett kissed her forehead. "Man, it's the perfect day for biking. You want to go for a ride?"

"I already did my hair." Floressa nestled into Barrett.

"What about you, Elsa? I bet you don't ride many motorcycles in Metzahg."

I looked away and blushed, just like Elsa would. "I'm fine."

"She can't go on a motorcycle with you!" Floressa's voice rose. "She'd have to hug you and get close. No girl gets near my man."

"Get your claws back." Barrett's eyes crinkled. "Besides,

Elsa's been in love with Karl since they were two. She's practically my sister. One quick spin? The hills here are awesome."

"No, seriously, I'm good."

Barrett finally made eye contact with me. "Really fast. I'll show you some evergreen trees in the area."

EVERGREEN. Gah, I was an idiot. This wasn't Barrett, this was Reed, and he'd found a perfect excuse for us to be alone to talk. He'd been so in character, so Barrett, I hadn't realized that this was a Sproutville boy in front of me. The boy I kind of had a crush on, who had his arm around one of the most gorgeous model/actress/heiress/princesses in the world. He'd kissed her, too, and not a dunk tank or stage kiss. That was major beet action. "Oh. Wow. I really love evergreen trees. I guess I could, even if you aren't Karl."

Floressa made a pouty face. "Okay, take her. We just had a big-girl talk anyway, and she probably needs some time to think about why she's here. Right, Elsa?"

"No I don't."

"Yes you do!" Floressa tapped me on the head. "Don't you get it? I get what I want, one way or the other. So you might as well make it easy for us both."

"Floressa—"

"Now, go look at those stupid trees with my boyfriend so he'll be happy. And don't go thinking you can switch princes. *That* Fenmar boy is mine."

Barrett was already walking to the front door. We followed him outside, and there on the circular driveway was a black motorcycle. I didn't know a thing about motorcycles, but it looked expensive. Barrett/Reed handed me a pink helmet and threw his leg over the side of the bike. I hesitated. I knew this was a great opportunity for us, but my safety-scared father would die if he knew I was getting on one of these things. I shot Floressa a look. She was giggling.

"Never mind. She's scared. I totally want to see this."

Barrett revved up the engine. "See you in fifteen minutes, babe. And have the chef take those nasty beet salads away and make us some real food. Something with meat. You're too skinny."

Floressa stuck her tongue out at Barrett. I squeezed in behind him and wrapped my arms loosely around him "You're going to need to hold on tighter than that," he said. I could barely hear him over the roar of the motorcycle. "Just pretend we're on my tandem bike touring Sproutville."

It was the perfect thing to say. This was exactly what I needed to do and where I needed to be. I squeezed Reed harder, and we were off.

Floressa blew a kiss from the driveway. Reed waved, then turned the corner. "There's a park a few blocks away," he said. "Let's go there and it'll give us some time to talk."

"Yeah, I have news," I said.

"So do I." Reed leaned into the right turn as we drove uphill. "I might have found our lost sub."

A few well-dressed kids toddled through the sandbox while their nannies fed them organic snacks. Reed and I sat on the swing set, a seat apart from each other, in case a roving paparazzo spotted two royals together who were actually *together* with other people.

Reed managed to keep Barrett's usual bored expression on his face as he shared the details. "So I looked online and hired a detective to find all the women named Caprice in Hollywood who are also actresses."

"Seriously? We've only been here for an hour or so."

"I'm not the one babysitting Floressa. It was easy. I also figured Caprice needed to be between twenty-five and forty-five if she subbed when Meredith was a Watcher. And Meredith said the sub was Italian, right?"

"Yeah, Caprice left Italy after Façade kicked her out. Not that she remembers that."

"Well, we found four girls named Caprice who fit that description."

"That's awesome!" I jumped off the swing. "Let's go visit them now."

Reed shook his head. "They live all over the valley—we wouldn't have time to see one. Besides, Façade's going to get suspicious if we're running around meeting a bunch of girls with the same name. We have to get them together somehow."

A kid kicked a ball by us, and his nanny came over to retrieve it. She had a magazine in her hand. I'd bought the same copy. Barrett was on the cover with Floressa. She bent over, picked up the ball, and when she looked up at Barrett, froze. "You're a prince," she squeaked.

Reed grinned. "Guilty."

"Did you buy a home here? Oh my gosh, my employer loves you."

"Just visiting."

"Can you sign my magazine?"

Reed patted his leather jacket for a pen. "Sure." He scribbled his name across the top. I had no idea what Barrett's signature really looked like. That was a good thing for a Match to practice.

He handed the magazine back to her and she clutched it to her chest. "This so beats meeting that soap opera star last week. Everyone will die of jealousy when they hear I met a prince!" She ran over to the other nannies, who looked up sharply at Barrett and me.

"Guess we should go," he grumbled.

"Hey, wait. Think about what she just said."

"That I'm a prince. Yeah."

"No, bringing the Caprices together." I smacked my leg. "I'm supposed to add people to the wedding guest list for Floressa. So I'll add all these Caprices too. It's a party hosted by an Academy Award winner. A struggling actress would kill for that invite."

"Brilliant."

I gave a mock curtsy. "I try."

"I can't believe Floressa put you in charge of something like guest-list additions."

"It gets worse," I lowered my voice. "She wants me to ruin the wedding."

Reed's eyes bugged. "You're kidding. Why would she want you to do that?"

"Because she doesn't want to go live in Tharma, among other reasons."

"What are you going to do?"

"Talk her out of it, I guess. It wasn't the kind of plotting I had in mind."

Reed grabbed my wrist, excited. My skin tingled with energy. "Not what you had in mind, but it's perfect!"

"No way. Too many people would be hurt."

"Don't *really* ruin the wedding. Just let Floressa think you are."

"What? Why?"

Reed dropped my wrist and strode over to his motorcycle. I hurried after him.

"This will be the perfect way to distract Floressa. Look, I'll take care of contacting the Caprices and getting them into the wedding along with Floressa's extra invite list."

"But Floressa told me *I* had to."

"That's because she thinks I'm Barrett and doesn't want to involve him." Reed waved at the nannies standing at the edge of the grass staring at us. "You keep Floressa happy and brainstorm questions to ask the Caprices."

"Hey, remember how you said there is an application on the manual that can tell if someone is a sub?"

"Yeah. I haven't used it yet. But this girl isn't a sub anymore."

"But maybe there's a little trace of magic left and

it'll show up on the radar. It's worth trying, right?"

Reed glanced back at the nannies. "It wouldn't hurt. Might help narrow down somehow."

"Exactly," I said. "Final question. What do we do when we know we have the right girl?"

"I don't know. Find a way to make her remember?"

"But she had her memory washed."

"Hey, I found the girls. You work out that part." He handed me my helmet. "We have to get back. That nanny just pulled out her camera phone."

He shoved his helmet over his head before the nannies had a chance to get a decent shot. We zipped down the hills and back into Floressa's driveway. He parked the bike and jumped off. "Hurry. Floressa's going to give me grief if we're gone too long."

My stomach flipped. He was certainly in a rush to get back to her. I wondered how many times Reed had subbed for Barrett, how many times he'd seen Floressa. How many times he'd kissed her. No, I didn't want to know the answer to that.

Floressa ran out to meet us. "Des—Elsa. Ryder's here. Emergency. He wants to do a color analysis on you, stat. I think you're a summer, but he swears you're a winter. Come on!"

I turned to Reed, but he was already getting back on the motorcycle. He revved his engine. "Have fun, girls. Big day coming up."

Chapter 22

ow that Floressa thought I was on board with her plan to ruin the wedding, we got along much better. And I would never publicly admit this, but the next two days of whirlwind planning and scheming with Floressa was, well . . . It was fun. Floressa had this way of sucking you into her world, until you got to this point where it almost felt normal to design four dresses for one party. I let myself get into the glitter and glam because if I sat down for one second, my stomach pitted up with the epic task ahead of me, both with Floressa and with Caprice.

The night before the wedding, Floressa and I shoe shopped in her bedroom. A salesman from an elite boutique had set up hundreds of shoes in our sizes. I was trying on a pair of green sandals that cost more than my dad's car when Gina came into the room, glowing and grinning. "Flossie! There you girls are. Are you prepared for the party tomorrow?"

Floressa rolled her eyes. "I already told her about the wedding, Mom."

"Honey, stop blabbing!" Gina offered me an encouraging smile. "Not that I think you'll tell anyone, dear, but I've gone to such great lengths to keep this secret. My publicist doesn't even know."

"Don't worry. I'm royal—I understand the importance of secrecy."

She squeezed my shoulder. "Thank you. I can't tell you how giddy I am about tomorrow."

"It's your fourth wedding." Floressa yawned.

"Well, my first marriage was to the king, and since we're getting married again, I'll count it as three."

"That's like Elizabeth Taylor and Richard Burton," I said.

"Who?" Floressa asked.

"They were, like, the biggest Hollywood couple of the sixties," I said. "She was married eight times, twice to Richard Burton."

"Do you watch a lot of old movies on your farm?" Floressa asked, confused.

Nope. Elsa probably does not. I examined my new manicure. "I, er, read about it in some Elizabeth Taylor tribute piece."

"Well, third time's the charm for me," Gina said. "Aung is it. I've never been so happy in my life."

Floressa didn't say anything.

"He's a lucky man," I said.

Gina brushed her hand along Floressa's hair. "And Floressa will have a father, and a sister, and a title. It's a wonderful package deal. We're all lucky."

"Oooh, look at these ones!" Floressa dove for a pair of gold pumps. "Perfect!"

Gina laughed. "Well, I'll let you girls get back to your shopping. Floressa, I e-mailed you some ideas for your toast."

"I'm not doing a toast," Floressa said.

"Well, in case you change your mind," Gina said, the pain clear in her voice.

I waited until Gina was gone to hit Floressa with my sandal. "Why are you so mean to her?"

"Oh, please. She's ruining my life. Let's not get into it."

"But did you see how excited she was about your dad? She's totally in love."

"She was in love with her last two husbands, too. Trust me, it's not going to last." She checked her watch. "So, what have you figured out for the wedding-ruining stuff?"

Under any other circumstance, I would run out and tell Gina what Floressa was planning. It physically hurt, knowing I might be a part of causing someone grief. And worse, I couldn't feel one molecule of magic when subbing for Floressa, because I couldn't relate to her in this situation. I didn't feel bad for her, or want to understand her better. Zippo empathy.

What I wanted to do was slap her. But only after she gave me the new shoes.

"You really want to go through with this?" I asked.

"Yes," Floressa said firmly. "That's why you're here. So. Ideas?"

"I had one."

Floressa dragged me over to her bed and propped herself on her elbows. "Spill."

"I wrote up a press release about the wedding," I said slowly. "If we send it out, every major news source will be all over the story. The privacy will be blown, and your mom will call it off."

"For now. She'll just do another ceremony later."

"What, do you want me to make your parents break up forever and hate each other?"

"Not hate each other." Floressa chewed on her lip and looked away. "Just never want to get married. Seriously, my life will be a nightmare. Living with a new family I don't know in a new country I don't like. That can't happen."

"I can't make them fall out of love. Even magic can't override that."

"Fine. Magic, shmagic. But we'll wait to send out the press release until right before the ceremony. I still want the party. And one more important question."

"What?" I asked wearily.

She pointed to the shoes. "Gold or silver?"

The next morning, I found Floressa surrounded by a flurry of makeup artists and hairdressers. The ceremony was at a private ranch in the mountains outside of Malibu. Gina and the king had already gone up for final preparations, and Floressa, Barrett, and I were supposed to meet them in three hours. Which meant crunch time for the Floressa team. Ryder, her main stylist, was trying to sew Floressa into her purple mini-dress, but she wasn't cooperating. Surprise.

I handed Floressa the two sheets of paper that I'd printed out that morning.

"What are these?" she asked. "Don't make me read. I have enough to worry about today."

"You don't want me reading those out loud," I said.

"Ouch! Ryder!" she screamed. "That's the fifth time you've poked me."

"It's the eighteenth time you've moved," Ryder said through a mouthful of pins. "Numbers are still in your favor. Now, what is this? A script?"

Floressa scrunched up her nose as she read the two sheets. "This"—she pointed to the first sheet—"is brilliant. The other thing you can just throw away, because I'm not going to need it." She crumpled the paper and threw it on the ground.

I dove for the sheet and smoothed it out. "Just in case you change your mind."

"I won't."

"You might."

"I WILL NOT!" Floressa's face went red.

The room quieted. Ryder held up a hand, and the rest of the makeup crew fled the room. He spit the pins out of his mouth and stood so he was towering over Floressa. "Do you know how splotchy your skin gets when you're hysterical? Do you?"

Floressa grabbed a pillow and hid her face.

"Do I need to pull out *Celebrity Insider* and show you the picture at Ashleigh Vickerson's fashion show where you got upset and SPLOTCHED UP THE PAGE?"

Floressa lowered her pillow. "No."

"Good," Ryder said. "Now, Your Highness."

"Which highness?" Floressa asked. "We're *both* princesses, remember?"

Ryder shot her a murderous look. "Princess Elsa. Can this wait for later?"

"Just giving Floressa what she asked for." I gave Floressa a pointed look. "It's up to you what you do with that. I haven't sent that release to anyone. I also e-mailed it to you, along with contacts, so *you* can send it out when you're ready. If you feel good about it."

Floressa picked at her skirt. "I don't feel good about any of this. It's lose-lose."

"Doesn't have to be." I nudged her with the sheet of paper she'd crumpled. "Just hold on to this."

Floressa folded both pieces of paper and tucked them into her bejeweled clutch. "Fine. I'll think about it. Sheesh, who's paying you to be my conscience anyway?"

Ryder looked at both of us and shook his head. "Paying? If this is some royal code, I don't speak it. But I do speak fashion, and we need to get you in your outfit, Princess Elsa. Floressa, will you be all right for fifteen minutes?"

Floressa was staring off into space. She shook her head like she was trying to shake off our conversation. I knew

Floressa was good, deep down. DEEP deep down. I still hoped she wouldn't send that press release, still hoped she'd support her mom instead. "Just make sure you leave an hour for us to finalize accessories," she said.

"At least," Ryder said. He led me into an adjourning guest room, which was being used as a makeshift changing room. Hanging on a hanger was the most spectacular aqua dress I'd ever seen. "For me?"

Ryder took a step back. "A little ice queeny, but you are a winter, and aqua is just too hot right now."

"I love it," I whispered, fingering the delicate fabric.

"That's the first positive thing I've heard today," Ryder said. "Someone needs to slap that girl back to her senses."

"I would if I could."

Ryder giggled. "You and me both. Now slip that little number on and let's make sure the measurements are right."

I changed in the bathroom. Elsa looked stunning in jammies, so this dress made her absolutely . . .

"Ethereal." Ryder gasped when I came back. "You will walk up to every camera at that party and tell them it is a Ryder Sullivan original, understand? That dress will be the highlight of my spring season."

Even though he wasn't talking about me, I blushed. "Thanks. I just hope Floressa approves."

"She won't."

"What?" The last thing I needed today was to have Floressa mad at me because of my clothes. "Why? Is she wearing aqua later?"

"Oh, honey. Ryder Sullivan does NOT duplicate his color palette at the same event! No, Floressa doesn't like to be outshined. It's a good thing you're dating Barrett's brother, because otherwise she would not let you NEAR her boy looking that good."

"What? Oh, I don't like Barrett—"

"That's what I'm saying. But still, little advice, stay back. Going on a motorcycle ride when you're all grungy is one thing, but that dress . . . now I'm wondering if I went too far." Ryder's phone rang. "Speaking of. I better go check that she's not burning that paper. What'd you do, add her to a not-hot list?"

"I wish I could tell you," I said. "You might want to give her a little pep talk on wedding etiquette, though."

Ryder gave me a confused look and closed the door. I turned and looked at myself/Elsa in the mirror one last time. Despite all the attached drama, I felt a little bad that she was missing this. She deserved to know what it felt like to wear a dress this beautiful.

There was a knock on the door. I called out, "Did you find me a diamond necklace, Ryder?"

"Oh, now you're stealing jewels?" The door opened, and standing in front of me was a very angry looking Prince Karl. His face softened for a moment when he saw Elsa in her dress, but he shook it off.

My heart stopped. Like, no beats happened. No breathing happened. My blood froze in my body and I just stood there, everything suspended. So maybe I did still like him, a little. Or maybe I was just really in character as Elsa. Either way, Prince Karl was not who I'd expected to see walk through the door. "Karl?"

"Yes, lovely to meet you." Karl checked his watch. "Now I think you need to give up my girlfriend's identity before you mess up her whole life. If you have any decency."

Barrett skidded past the door, completely out of breath. "Meet . . . Karl. He . . . came back a little . . . early. Must have wanted . . . to see . . . evergreen trees."

"Evergreen," I repeated faintly. So Reed was still here. And now, here was the real Karl. My two crushes, side by side. Oh, boy.

"And the jig is up." Karl pushed Reed's hand off his shoulder. "I ran into my idiot brother at the resort and found out he'd ditched so he didn't have to attend Gina and Aung's royal wedding. Of course, Elsa had no idea she had booked a sub during such an important time. So I switched with my sub and got the first flight to L.A. to see what was happening myself. Elsa would be here, but Nana Helga wanted to stay at the resort. Plus, Elsa said she knew Desi . . . That's your name, right?"

I nodded. He knew my name. This was so weird.

"Well, she said Desi was a good person and that you wouldn't do anything to harm her. Now I hear from Barrett's sub that you're trying to ruin a wedding, and Elsa will be the one to take the blame." Karl snorted. "Sometimes Elsa is a little too trusting."

"Now, hold on here," Reed said. "I didn't say Desi was

trying to ruin the wedding. I said she was trying to stop Floressa from ruining the wedding—"

"I don't want to hear from you, either." Karl scowled at Reed. "You're in on this too. Why would Floressa ruin her own mum's wedding? I'm going to go have a talk with Floressa, fix this mess, and make sure my girlfriend's reputation stays intact."

"Girlfriend?" I asked, finally finding my voice. "Really, is Elsa, like, officially your girlfriend now?"

Karl gave me a weary look. "What does that have to do with anything?"

"Nothing." I swallowed. I *could* point out that I was a big reason that Karl even had Elsa as a girlfriend, thank you, and now he was repaying me with a bunch of uninformed accusations. "Look, you're going to stop yelling at us right now. We are helping, and I do NOT appreciate your tone. Got that, Prince Karl?"

Both boys looked at me with shocked expressions. Crazy—they looked so . . . brotherly next to each other.

"Do you really think I would risk my job or hurting Elsa's reputation and Floressa's parents' happiness by ruining this wedding? Seriously?"

"Well, yes," Karl said sheepishly. "I thought—"

"The only one who would ruin this wedding is Floressa— that's her choice, and I can't force her to do anything that she doesn't want to do. I've told her I will help her with a few other requests. Barrett, or Fake Barrett, is in charge of adding some of Floressa's friends to the guest list. Fine. As for me,

I'm going to stay near Floressa in the hopes that she doesn't tell the press about the event, and if she does, I'll do damage control. Elsa would do the same thing, wouldn't she?"

Karl's face reddened. "Well, I suppose, given the circumstances, she might—"

"And you, Karl." I couldn't help it; when I said his name, I lost the edge in my voice. I would always have a soft spot for Karl. He was my first prince, really, despite all the identity mix-ups along the way. He was trying to be noble for Elsa, and I loved that about him. "Karl, your job is to act normal and stay out of our way. And trust us, okay? Do you think you can do that for me?"

"I think . . ." Karl looked down at his casual white button-down shirt and dark jeans. "I think I need to find some more formal attire."

"Do that. Now, if you'll excuse me, I need to finish getting ready. Run along, boys."

Karl shuffled out of the room. Reed stood there, staring at me in wonder.

"What?" I asked. "Look, I know Elsa looks hot in this dress, but—"

"I'm not thinking about Elsa." He rubbed the back of his neck. "You're so . . . You've come a long way from that girl I met at Idaho Potato Days. Remind me never to cross you, okay?"

"Reed, never cross me."

He grinned, which looked very Reed-like even on Barrett's adorable face, and punched my arm. "Okay, princess. Get your tiara on. It's showtime."

229

Chapter 23

We took a limo to the ranch. Karl was sitting right next to me, and across from us were Floressa and Reed/Barrett. Floressa was snuggled in close to Reed. Another limo could fit in the space between Karl and I.

"I still don't get why you're here, Karl," Floressa said. She'd been rude to him ever since he showed up. Of course, she thought this was Karl's sub, because the real Karl was supposed to be at the resort with Elsa. "Shouldn't you be in Fenmar? Or vacationing somewhere?"

"I asked him to come to lend me support," Reed said. "So I could have, uh, more support to offer you."

Floressa nestled into Reed's shoulder. "Don't I have the best boyfriend, Elsa?"

I barely managed to avoid an eye roll. "Sure."

"I love you Bear-Bear."

Reed grinned.

I opened the mini-fridge and looked for a Mountain Dew, anything to avoid watching those two together. I bet Reed loved his job. He can say he doen't like Floressa all he wants, but seriously, she's *Floressa Chase*.

"So, you've obviously subbed for Elsa before," Karl said softly.

"I have in the past." I scooted across the seat so we could talk. "I like her a lot. I'm happy for you two."

Karl couldn't help but smile. "Thank you. Yes, she is remarkable. When did you say you subbed for her?"

Karl wanted to know if I'd ever subbed for her when they were together. Façade created an invisible barrier between royals, an unspoken secret. They all knew that they used subs, but no one ever knew *when*. It had probably never occurred to Karl before that the girl he was dating wasn't always Elsa. "I subbed for her in Metzahg. Right before Nana Helga allowed her to join the royal scene."

"Metzahg?" Karl's face reddened. "Er, do you know . . . what dates, exactly?"

"Not really." Of course I did. I'd only replayed that trip a million times in my head. But now that I knew Reed wasn't Karl's sub, I had no clue what moments were spent with Karl and what time was with another sub.

"You two are getting snuggly!" Floressa laughed. "Ooh, are you going to kiss?"

"We're not ones for public displays of affection," Karl said smoothly.

Floressa thought this was fun because she was making two subs very uncomfortable. Then again, she also thought the boy sitting next to her was really Prince Barrett, so what did she know?

The limo stopped and Floressa clapped her hands. "We're here! Come on. There's a party to get to!"

The door opened and Floressa stepped out.

"Ladies first," Reed said.

I followed Floressa and looked out at the spectacular view. The word "ranch" had thrown me. The green mountains rose on one side of us and dropped off at a cliff over the ocean. The mansion sprawled across the picturesque scene, and white tents were already filled with tables and elaborate silver-and-blue decorations.

"Now, this is a winter wonderland," I said.

Reed stood behind me. "Not in Idaho anymore, huh?"

We picked our way up the pathway.

Floressa glanced behind her shoulder. "I'll meet up with you in a bit. I want to tell my mom congratulations first."

So Floressa was softening. Maybe she would choose to support her mom, which would make my job here a lot easier. I gave her hand a quick squeeze. "Find me when you're done."

When she was gone, Reed readjusted his tie. "Hey, Karl, why don't you come with me? I've got to go talk the bouncer into extending the guest list, and Barrett didn't leave his wallet."

"You need my money?" Karl asked incredulously.

"It's for a worthy cause. Come on." Reed leaned in to me and whispered, "We'll scope out the guests next to the entrance. Can you watch the people arriving and see if any of them are a Caprice?"

"How will I know?"

"They'll probably look out of place. You can also try the sub scanner app."

They hurried away, leaving me standing near the first entrance as guest after guest brushed past me. It was like standing on the red carpet at the Oscars. I recognized nearly every face, some from the movies, others from royal gossip magazines. Hailey Gonzalez, teen superstar, even stopped me. "Oh! I'm so excited to meet you, Your Highness. I've been following you and Prince Karl in every magazine. Are you here together?"

I shook my head, thunderstruck. "*You're* excited to meet *me?*"

"Of course. And that dress is to die for. I heard aqua was the new teal."

I gave myself fifteen more minutes to mingle. Fifteen minutes to fulfill both my acting dreams and royal delights. I would carry that up close people-watching moment with me forever. Or at least until Façade wiped my memory.

I noticed one girl right when she got out of her car, a beat-up VW bug. Her eyes were huge as she took in the country singer to her left.

"Hi!" I said. "I'm Elsa. Who are you?"

"Caprice. One word. I'm an actress."

Her accent sounded like she was from New York, not another country, but actresses were always changing their accents.

"Where are you from?" I asked.

"Staten Island." She chomped on a piece of gum. "Look, I got an invitation, so I'm supposed to be here. Stop interrogating me, got it?"

I backed away. Meredith had said Caprice's emotion was kindness. There was nothing magical or nice coming from this woman. But, then again, people change, and she could have hardened since working at Façade.

I clicked onto the sub-scanner application, and I discreetly held my manual behind Caprice, one word, to see if anything happened. The red and green bars that were supposed to increase if there was any magic didn't move. Although we knew old subs might not register, it confirmed my gut feeling that this wasn't my girl.

"Well, have fun at the party," I said.

"Yeah, whatever." Her jaw dropped. "OMG, is that Floressa Chase walking over here? That's Floressa Chase!"

Floressa stumbled down the lawn toward us. It wasn't until she got closer that I could see that she was crying.

"Floressa Chase is coming to talk to me. Move out of my way."

Caprice pushed me to the side and waved at Floressa. Floressa gave her a look of bewilderment before grabbing me in a hug. "Des . . . Els . . . can we talk for a second?"

"Sure, sure." I gave Caprice a little smile—seriously, she better not be the sub—and led Floressa into a garage. "What's wrong?" I asked.

Floressa started to cry harder, her makeup smudging. "I didn't mean to."

"Didn't mean to what?"

"I sent the e-mail."

My heart sank. "What e-mail?"

"Don't 'what e-mail?' me. The press release. I sent it out to all the contacts you listed."

"Are you kidding me?"

"I didn't mean to!" she wailed. "I got on the house computer, and I was just reading the press release one more time. And then Isla came in and was all bouncy and happy and going on how she's so excited to have a new mom, but Gina is *my* mom. She's always been my mom, and it's just been us two, and now she loves my dad, and she . . . she probably loves him more, and it's not only us anymore, and . . . it's like everything went black except for the computer screen, and I clicked the mouse. One little click, Desi, and boom . . . e-mail to ten magazines. And I regretted it right away, I promise. I . . . I'm awful. I'm an awful person. Who gets mad at her mom for being happy?"

"Oh, Floressa." I handed her a tissue and my Rouge compact mirror. She wiped furiously at the makeup that had taken hours to apply. I couldn't handle this girl sometimes. She was selfish, rude, childish, self-absorbed . . . and relatable. Floressa couldn't be more different than me, but in this situation, I understood her. Change is hard. Change in your family? Probably the hardest. I'd been a brat to my parents when Gracie was first born, even though I loved her, and I had a moment of odd jealousy when my mom told me about this new baby. Floressa didn't have many people in her life that liked her for her, who really tried to understand her like Gina did. All this wedding scheming wasn't so much about trying to mess up her parents' lives, but about keeping things as they were.

"You know love is like the strongest force in the world, right?" I asked.

"Yeah, I know. No matter what, my mom and dad are still going to get married."

"They are. But no matter what, your mom is still going to love you, Floressa. Even if she loves other people. And your dad and Isla are going to love you. They already do. You're not losing here, you're gaining."

Floressa kicked at a red sports car parked in the garage. "Well, that's all great. But what am I supposed to do *now*? All those helicopters are going to show up."

"You'll have to warn your mom—tell her what you did."

"You mean, take responsibility for my actions?"

"Yeah."

"But that's why I have *you* here." Floressa tugged on my arm. "Can't you say you sent out the press release? So my mom doesn't have to get mad at me?"

"Oh, so Elsa can get in trouble? No, Floressa, this is on you."

Floressa drew in a shaky breath. "Yeah, okay. You're right. I'm supposed to meet her in the front entryway so I can walk her out. They're doing the ceremony on the cliff."

"Walk her out?"

"Like, down the aisle." She gritted her teeth. "This is going to be the worst conversation EVER. I'm not paying you double anymore, I hope you know that."

We linked arms and walked back onto the field. Floressa kept her head down as we hurried up to the house. We were almost to the back steps when King Aung stepped out onto the balcony of the mansion wearing his military uniform, medals and all. The chatter around us died down as one by one the guests noticed the king and turned to stare. It's not every day someone dresses up in military duds. Only for big events. Like weddings. "Friends and family. Gina Chase requests you join her on the north cliff for a very special surprise. Thank you."

The crowd buzzed. I smiled encouragingly at Floressa. "Looks like your mom will be waiting for you. You want a second alone before I come in?"

"Yes, I'm going to need to figure out what to say. Unless you want to tell my mom—"

"Floressa."

"Right. Okay. Going in." Floressa squared her shoulders and walked up the back steps. The break gave me two or three minutes to find Reed and recoup. With all the Floressa drama, I hadn't had time to hunt out more Caprices, and now . . . who knows? They might call off the wedding and send everyone home. We might be out of time altogether.

Reed was under one of the tents, talking with Karl. He waved at me and rushed against the tide of people now wandering over to the cliff. Chairs were being whisked out, an aisle formed. Ryder fluttered around with rose petals.

"Hey. Evergreen," he said.

"Evergreen," I confirmed.

"I talked to two of the Caprices before the Prince of Spain yanked me away to discuss polo."

"And?"

"Not our girls. One lady was fifty and from Norway. I don't even know how she made the detective's list. The other Caprice had an Italian accent and could have been the right age, but I ran my manual over her and there wasn't a trace of magic. Not a lick. I know we said that application might not be accurate, but I just had a feeling about her, like maybe she wasn't smart enough to have worked for Façade? Or didn't have that special something, you know?"

"I felt the same way about Staten Island."

"Who?"

"The third Caprice. She goes by only her first name."

Ryder had stopped showering rose petals and was pointing at us frantically to take our seats.

"So that's three," I said. "Do you know if the last girl showed up?"

"No. But her name's on the list. I'm sure she wouldn't miss it. We'll have the rest of the wedding to find her."

"We might be leaving sooner than planned," I said.

The crowd was now sitting in the seats, a harpist setting up in front. A large canopy was being assembled, with flowers being rushed in by frantic florists. The guests were beginning to understand what was happening, and all were craning their necks back to the house. "Floressa told the press about the wedding—sort of by accident—and now she's confessing to her mom, but the leak means they might call off the wedding."

A whirring sound filled the air, and I instinctively reached for Reed's hand. "Oh, no! I've heard that sound before. It's a bubble."

Reed dropped my hand and pointed to the sky. "No. Rhymes with bubble, though. Trouble."

A helicopter. The press had arrived.

"We're not going to have time to find the other Caprice now!" I yelled. The guests were ducking or waving, based on their personal photo-opportunity policies.

"Go talk to Floressa. I'll see if I can find the sub. DO NOT get sent home until we talk to this girl, okay? And, Desi?"

"Yeah?"

"I want you to know, in case something happens, that . . . you're really . . . Never mind. I'll talk to you soon."

I didn't have time to think about what Reed was going to say to me. During my stealth training, I'd learned to push emotions away during times of crisis. I picked up the hem of Ryder Sullivan's original design and ran into the house. Gina was sitting at the bottom of the stairs in her wedding dress, sobbing, and Floressa was right next to her, analyzing her pedicure. I slipped into a chair by the door, not wanting to interrupt.

"I was so secretive!" Gina cried. "I don't know where the leak could be."

Floressa shrugged. "Probably the maid. Or the butler. Yeah, blame the butler."

The king rushed into the room and folded Gina into a hug. "What do you want to do?"

"I don't . . . I don't know. Everything is ruined."

Floressa played with the sleeve of her dress. She finally looked up at me and made eye contact. "Oh, fine." She stood up, casting a guilty glance at her parents. "So, I told the press."

The king's face hardened. Gina gasped. "Flossie, no! How could you?"

"I didn't mean to!" Floressa threw up her hands. "Well, I meant to, but I didn't really *really* mean to. I just wanted things to stay how they were. I thought if you got married, my life would be over."

"Don't you want us to be together?" King Aung asked gently. "Finally?"

"I do. I mean, I sort of do." Floressa wiped at a tear. "Look, I don't care if we live here or in Tharma or Timbuktu. I don't want to lose my mom."

"Honey, you don't really think that, do you?" Gina stood and gave Floressa a hug. "I love you very much. Even when you sabotage my wedding."

"Fourth wedding," Floressa grumbled.

Gina laughed and smoothed out her daughter's hair. King Aung joined them in the hug, and they just stood there, crying. My heart went out to the king and Gina. Even to Floressa. She wasn't being a spoiled brat. She was a scared brat, and that at least made her more sympathetic. And made me *empathetic*.

"I promise I didn't want this to happen. I'm so sorry," Floressa said. "I let it go too far. But I did write a toast." Floressa shot a look at me. "I didn't even read the one you gave me, Elsa. I wrote one all on my own."

My fingers and toes tingled. I wanted to create a force field around the ranch to keep the helicopters away, to use superhero strength or to magically, MAGICALLY, make everything better.

But I couldn't. Why did it take me so long to realize that? Nothing had changed since the last time I'd subbed for Floressa. My magic wasn't about pulling a rabbit out of a hat. Yes, magic made floating bubbles possible, and physical transformation, and even time travel. But that was combined magic, taken from former subs and the earth and animals and . . . everywhere. My MP, my magic, was an emotion. A talent. That's why I hadn't been able to zap Kylee with a love potion—sometimes the most important thing you can do, the most magical thing, is to show someone you understand. That you care. And my ability was not only to understand others, but to help them. My magic really was to make an impact. And right now all that entailed was getting a family together. Literally. And figuratively.

The words felt so right when they came out. "You can still get married," I said.

Everyone turned around and stared at me.

"Right here. In this hallway if you want. The helicopters can't get in the house. And this glass skylight could be your canopy. And Isla can be the flower girl and Floressa can read her toast and . . . just you. Just your family."

"Just our family," the king repeated.

"She's right!" Floressa raced over to me. "I could bring in Isla and the rabbi."

The king and Gina exchanged a look. "It'd still be nicer than our first wedding," the king said with a chuckle.

"But what about the people?" Gina asked. "And my family, and the celebrities, and the dignitaries? What do we tell them?"

"They'll be fine," Floressa said. "They came for a party; we can still give them a party. There's food and music. They can eat cake."

"Visit with them afterward. You just don't want pictures of your ceremony, right?" I asked.

"True." The king shook his head. "I'm sorry, but what are you doing in here?"

"She's my friend," Floressa said. "Sort of."

King Aung shrugged and squeezed Gina's waist. "What do you think?"

"I think . . ." Gina smiled at her daughter and her ex/soon-to-be husband. "Let's do the ceremony right here. Right now."

Chapter 24

The rabbi and Isla were brought in quickly. Meanwhile, Ryder and the wedding planner took over removing the folding chairs and decorations. And the guests did just what Floressa had suggested. Ate cake. Gluten-free, low-fat cake.

It actually worked out to my advantage. Now I had time to grab Reed and hunt down this sub. But not too much time. Floressa and company would be out soon, and she would want Barrett by her side.

Reed and Karl were near the five-foot snowflake ice sculpture. Karl's eyes lit up when he saw me, but clouded over when he remembered I wasn't really his girlfriend. "Elsa. Where's Floressa?" Karl asked.

"They're doing the ceremony inside; just them," I said.

"Should I go in there?" Reed asked.

"No, stay out here with the evergreen trees," I said.

Reed and Karl gave me a weird look. "What would he care about trees right now?" Karl asked.

"Are they coming out after?" Reed asked.

"I don't know. Why don't you come with me, though, and we can talk more about those EVERGREEN trees."

Reed looked at Karl. "Uh, brude. Why is your girlfriend trying to show me trees? Is this some weird Metzahg pick-up line?" He winked at me. "Not that I'm complaining, but Floressa might get a little hostile."

Karl shook his head. "This isn't my girlfriend."

"You two broke up? Elsa, did you look at yourself in that dress and realize you're too good for my brother?"

I tried to smile, but I wanted to cry. This wasn't Reed. Barrett—the real Barrett—was back, along with Prince Karl. Elsa would surely be returning soon, too. We were SO close to finding that sub, and now I'd have to do it alone.

I couldn't do this alone. Not without Reed. Reed was the one who was so confident, who made this whole thing happen. He also was the one who knew more about magic, so he could figure out what to do with this vial and Caprice.

But if I didn't try, we might never get another chance like this. No, this was our *only* chance. Reed had risked so much to help me that I couldn't let his absence slow me down. I needed to be as brave as he thought I was.

"I'm, uh, helping Floressa," I said to Barrett. "How long have you been at the party?"

"All day."

"She's a substitute." Karl rolled his eyes. "And she knows you were using a sub too, right when your girlfriend was in crisis, nonetheless."

"Hey! I'm not heartless. I came back, right? I've been here for oh, five minutes now." Barrett slapped his brother on the back. "Hey, so if she's a sub, can you still kiss her?"

"I have to go," I said. "Prince Karl, any idea when Elsa is coming back?"

"She said she'd stay to give you a chance to work things out for Floressa. Looks like you did, so I'd imagine soon."

"Great. Thanks." This was where my training with Vanna came into play again. All my worry about Reed being gone had to be forgotten. We had a plan. Feelings were pushed away so I could accomplish our goal.

I hurried toward the entrance and the bouncer. He checked off people when they entered the party, so I could see if the other Caprice ever showed. If I still had time. Once Floressa's family walked out of the house, Elsa would want to come back and be with Karl for the party. I was rounding the corner of the house when I ran into a woman in a short brown dress.

"Oof!" I slammed into the wall, scratching my shoulder, but thankfully did not rip Ryder's dress. "Sorry!"

"No, I'm sorry!" The woman held on to me so she

wouldn't topple on her peep-toe heels. "I'm so sorry! I was rushing in, and—"

I noticed the slightest tinge of an accent. "What's your name?"

"Oh, uh, Caprice. Are you okay? I'm so clumsy sometimes, and you look so beautiful."

How NICE of her to notice. "I'm fine. Where are you from, by the way?"

"What? Oh. Milan originally, but I've been in L.A. since I was fifteen." She fixed the strap on her dress and looked longingly at my outfit. "I love your dress. Who designed it?"

"Ryder Sullivan original. But that's not important—"

"Not important! I would die for a Ryder Sullivan." She lowered her voice. "Don't tell anyone, but I got this off the rack. My agent hasn't booked me a gig in months, and then I get this out-of-the-blue invitation to the biggest party of the year."

"Wedding. It's a wedding, actually."

Her eyes widened. "Gina Chase invited me to her wedding? How sweet of her. I always thought she was nice."

Nice and sweet. This was my girl. "Actually, no. I invited you."

She furrowed her brow. "And, I'm sorry, who are you?"

"Well, right now, I'm Princess Elsa of the House of Holdenzastein. But other times . . . Look. I know I'm asking you weird questions, but . . . can you tell me what your life was like before you moved to L.A.? In Italy?"

"I was fifteen." She looked at me strangely. "I did what

most teenagers do. Shopped, went to school. But then, for some reason, I decided more than anything I wanted to be an actress. So I auditioned—"

"What made you decide that? How did you know you wanted to act?"

"I'm sorry, Princess Elsa, but I'm still confused why you're asking me these questions."

"I promise I'll explain after."

"Then . . . well, I don't know. It's like I woke up one morning and everything changed—the way I viewed the whole world, but I didn't really know why, and I wanted to be someone else and . . . I don't know. No one has ever asked me this before."

This was her. This was Meredith's Caprice. There wasn't time for me to explain everything about Façade. I whisked out my manual and ran a scan over Caprice. The bar only went up three notches, but that was enough to confirm that she still had traces of her magic. I pulled the vial out of my purse. My heart pounded—the moment I'd been building to was here. "So, the reason I got you on the guest list today was because of this."

"What is that?" Caprice squinted. "Makeup?"

Holy cosmetics. That's it! MAKEUP. No drinking, shaking, or sprinkling the liquid. That's not how Façade worked. When they sanitized, they had the sub put on powder from a compact. When we changed identities, subs used Royal Rouge. If makeup was how they took the magic away, surely that was how they put the magic back too! "Yes. And it's created just for you. See, it has your name and everything."

Caprice took the vial and analyzed the label. "This reminds me of something. From when I was younger. Is it a vintage brand?"

"It's, like, especially designed for each wearer." Awesome, a spark of memory! "It's a moisturizing . . . gel. You just rub some on each cheek, and it's supposed to be the greatest thing for your skin ever."

"So, you're a princess and you want me to rub some weird goo on my cheek?"

Caprice stuck a finger in the gooey magic and sniffed. I couldn't believe it. I couldn't believe all the training, all the planning and plotting and road bumps, and this was finally the moment I'd been working up to since I found that sub-sanitation room. And as excited as I was, it also felt like that moment right before a car wreck—all adrenaline and tension and suspense. Everything I knew about returning magic was from Meredith, and she hadn't told me anything. Caprice could break out in hives or explode from, I don't know, magical overkill. Logically, this was a stupid, ridiculous, misguided risk.

But now that I was in the moment, my emotions were taking over. Every magical fiber in my body told me that Caprice would be fine, that I was doing the right thing. I pictured the instant when she reconnected with her magic like *Beauty and the Beast* or another epic fantasy cartoon. Right when you think Caprice is doomed, there is a twinkle of magic, then a glittering explosion . . . and Caprice would be whole, and we'd go run through a meadow of . . . of blossoms and unicorns! The land of magical freedom. Reed would meet us there, I'd jump on a unicorn with him, and we'd ride into the brilliant sunset.

"Princess Elsa?" Caprice held her finger in the air. "So you just want me to rub this stuff on? Then can I go in?"

"Yes! Sorry. I'm not usually so pushy with this stuff, but you know when you love a product, you just want to share it with everyone. Plus, I got you into the biggest event of your life, so you can trust me. Right?"

Caprice shrugged. "Whatever. I hope this doesn't stain." She patted a dot on each cheek. "Ooh, it tingles. Does that mean it's working?"

"Yes." I breathed out. And waited. She still looked like the same woman, now just with two spots of blue on each cheek. No unicorns were popping in to welcome her to the Land of Magical Freedom just yet. In fact, it seemed nothing was happening. I mean, a tingle? Woo-hoo, my mom's plumping lip gloss does that.

"Okay. Well, it's on." Caprice plucked a tissue from her purse and wiped her fingers. "Can I go into the wedding now?"

A cheer went up behind us. The king and Gina must have joined their guests. Elsa was going to be back any minute. And then I heard my manual beep with a one-word message from Meredith.

COMING.

I grabbed Caprice by her elbow. She wasn't being lifted

249

into the air with magical power; she wasn't even glowing. Seriously, something better happen soon. This was supposed to be her big moment. Heck, this was *my* big moment—I'd sacrificed everything to give Caprice back her magic, and now . . .

WHY WASN'T ANYTHING HAPPENING?

"My brain hurts." Caprice leaned against the wall. "And my skin feels like it's dancing. What was in that stuff?"

The air filled with the sound of whirring, but I knew this time it wasn't a helicopter. It was Meredith and her bubble, and I was officially out of time.

"Darling." Meredith marched out and pointed a finger at me. "The amount of trouble you have produced makes my head spin."

"The trouble *I* produced?" I fumed. "What about you shipping Reed off to Africa?"

"You're mad at me for that? That's supposed to help you with—" She noticed Caprice and sucked in her breath. "Is this her?"

"Yes."

"You really found her." Meredith tilted her head to the side. "Unbelievable."

"Did you . . . Did you just step out of a BUBBLE?" Caprice's eyes widened. "Am I hallucinating now?"

So she saw the bubble. That was something, right? Meredith said only people with MP can see the bubble, and if Caprice's magic was fully stripped, then now . . . now her magic was back? But why wasn't more happening?

"This is Meredith, Caprice. Do you remember her? She watched you when you did the trial audition for Façade."

"Was that a TV pilot? I don't know what you're talking about. My skin is really going bananas—I'm going to wash my face."

"She won't remember," Meredith said. "The magic can come back, but not the memories. It's an entirely different process."

"Magic?" Caprice asked. "I know I'm feeling strange, what with the bubble and . . . this feeling that's happening, but . . . did you say magic?"

Meredith's expression softened. "That was your magic you just put on, Caprice. It's going to make you feel strong, it's going to make you feel powerful, it's going to make everything in your life feel big. I wish I could tell you more now, but I can't." She grabbed my arm. "I have this magical misfit to take care of."

"Wait, but, Meredith, so she has magic, but she doesn't remember anything from before? I can't just leave her, then—doesn't she need to be trained again so she can sub and show Façade what she can really do?"

Meredith dragged me over to her bubble. "Desi, she was never cut out to be a sub. I was her Watcher, and truly, she was awful. Were you really trying to return her magic just so she could go back to Façade?"

"Yes! So I could prove to Façade that they were wrong—that they shouldn't take magic away. And then, if they see her doing better, they'll realize that subs should . . . should . . ."

"Façade was never going to listen to you. This wasn't about proving anything to them. You were proving something to yourself," Meredith said.

"Wait, so are you leaving?" Caprice called. "In that . . . in that bubble!"

"I'll find you again, Caprice!" I said. Meredith tried to push me into the bubble, but I ducked my head. I reached my arm out to Caprice. "I promise I'll find you. Only, I won't look like this anymore. My name will be Desi. And if you see a girl who looks like me, um, it's not me. I mean, I'm not her. . . . She's the real princess is what I mean, because I'm just a sub."

"Wait, you're not a princess, I have magic, and . . ." Caprice gingerly touched her cheek. "What did this makeup just do to my face?"

Meredith gave me one more shove, and we both slammed into her office's hardwood floors. We lay there, gasping and panting. Meredith rolled to her side. "We had to leave. Before Genevieve's assistant, Dominick, showed up. I didn't want him to be the one to deliver you."

I pressed my cheek against the cool floor and closed my eyes. "It doesn't matter. Nothing matters now. I did what I had to do."

"I can't believe you actually went through with it."

"What did you think was going to happen?" I opened my eyes. "You gave me the magic."

"I've had that magic in my purse for almost twenty years. I just mean . . . I can't believe you had the guts to give her back the magic."

"Lot of good it did." I pushed myself up into a sitting position. "She doesn't remember Façade."

"Is that really why you were trying to find her?"

"I don't know." I was Desi again, back to my gray peacoat and champagne cocktail dress. "I thought she'd get her magic and all my questions would be answered. Now she's just another random person with MP who doesn't know what to do with it." I paused. "Wait, why did you say Dominick was coming?"

"Because Genevieve is technically your agent now, but of course she couldn't come. And it's her job to deliver you. I pulled some strings to get here."

"Deliver me where?" I asked, already dreading the answer. "The ambassadorship? Is it my turn for that?"

"Your ambassadorship wasn't scheduled until next March. But that just went out the window."

"Court of Appeals?"

"No, darling, don't act dumb." Meredith patted my hand. "I have to bring you back so Façade can fire you."

Chapter 25

Six months ago, I would have argued. Six months ago, I would have cried. Six months ago . . . I wouldn't have dreamed of doing all the things I did on this last job. And today as I traveled in Meredith's bubble, probably for the very last time, I felt a strange sense of peace.

I'd proven that magic could be restored to its rightful owner. I didn't know what would happen to Caprice now—if the change would even help her—but I'd erased one of Façade's mistakes. At least for Caprice, I'd made a difference. It was too bad that I couldn't do the same for more forgotten subs.

Meredith busied herself around the office, periodically

wiping at her eyes and smoothing her suit. Finally, she joined me on the couch. "So was it worth it?" she asked.

"Let me see if Façade has a specialized torture chamber, and I'll get back to you on that."

"I can't believe you got as far as you did all by yourself without Façade intervening."

"I'm just that good." I shrugged, trying to hide my relief that she didn't mention Reed. Maybe they would never figure out that he'd been involved, and he could stay at Façade, especially now that there wasn't much more we could do for our cause.

The bubble landed. Meredith held out her hand. "I will be on the council, but you will be your own spokesperson. This is different than the Court of Appeals."

"How?"

"It's not a hearing." Meredith offered a feeble smile. "It's a sentencing, and open to all Façade employees. We haven't had one in decades, so there will probably be a lot of curious onlookers."

"Swell."

"I'll do what I can to make it painless."

"Do you mean that literally or figuratively?" I asked.

"Er . . . both."

I expected to step out in the dungeonlike hall, like the room I'd originally visited during my visit to the Court of Royal Appeals after Level One. And although this space certainly was dark and foreboding, I could tell we weren't in or near the Façade building anymore. The air was too dank, and there was pressure in my ears like we were underground. Instead of smooth stone walls, there were lines of bones and . . .

"Skulls?" I gasped. "Meredith, please tell me these are not old subs."

"This is Paris. We're in the catacombs."

"Why are they talking to me in a tomb instead of, I don't know, a nice office with a city view?"

"Flair for drama. Which reminds me." Meredith grabbed a lit torch from the wall. "Come on. It's not far."

If I really tried to stretch my optimism, I could take it as a good sign that I wasn't brought to the sanitation room first thing. I scrunched in my shoulders as we walked through the narrow space, careful not to look too closely at the walls. Which, of course, were not walls. They were skeletons. Façade had the intimidation factor down to a science.

The heaviness of the air lessened as we walked up an incline. The relief was short-lived, however, because we finally reached a large open hall. The doorway had crossbones with a sign saying ILLIS QUI INTRARE NON EFFUGIET.

"What does that mean?" I whispered.

"Latin," Meredith said solemnly. "Those who enter do not exit."

"Oh."

I knew Façade could do scary, but this place made Kylee's horror movies look like Disney cartoons. The room was lit by sinister torchlight. A long table stretched across the center of the space, and stone benches were built into the wall like an ancient amphitheater. The seats were full of onlookers, all wearing black masquerade masks. I could pick out Hank from his sneakers, and Ferdinand from the tweed jacket he always wore. Reed's parents were in the front row, his mom dabbing at her eyes under the mask. I swallowed. Reed was noticeably absent.

"What's with the masks?" I whispered to Meredith.

"Stupid tradition. Supposed to give the witnesses anonymity, but you can tell who everyone is."

The council—all unmasked, dressed in black robes, their hair color faded in the flickering light—sat on one side of the table. There were three chairs on the other side. Dominick was on the right, Lilith on the left, leaving the empty seat for me. Fun. Desi's doom sandwich.

Meredith took her seat with the council. Hundreds of pairs of eyes watched as I shuffled over to my spot. Dang, why couldn't my magical skill be invisibility?

Genevieve's voice bounced against the walls. Against the skulls. Did I mention those yet? "Have a seat, Desi. We won't draw this out."

I slumped into the seat, trying my best to not look at Lilith, whose grin was bigger than the skulls behind her.

Dominick stood and spoke, his voice clear and emotionless. "We are here for the sentencing of one Desi Bascomb. Miss Bascomb broke into a secure Façade room and used confidential information gathered both at the agency and through client interactions to try to overturn the agency. The council has decided a trial is not necessary.

She also has already been found guilty of the following acts."

I got a whiff of lavender perfume when Lilith stood next. Even in a room that reeked of decay, her perfume still made me gag. She rattled a paper and read down the list of offenses. "'Treason, insubordination, trespassing, espionage, rebellion, and sedition.' Any one act is punishable. Combined, Desi's actions are inexcusable." Lilith paused at the end. "And can I just say that I saw this coming a mile away. We saw similar behavior when Desi came before the Court of Royal Appeals, and I insisted at that time that she was bad news. As far as sentencing goes, it's a pity the guillotine is no longer an option." Lilith sighed, like she'd been cheated. "I recommend we do what we should have done to Desi after her Level One performance. Sanitation and magic removal. And perhaps a night spent here in the catacombs for good measure."

"Lilith," Meredith scolded, "we're not here to rehash past trials. Desi's crimes have been read. It is up to the council to decide on sentencing and you"—she narrowed her eyes—"are not a member of this council."

Lilith flopped into her chair like she'd been pushed. Dominick robotically sat down as well. The council stood one by one and exited the room. The onlookers remained as we waited, silently, for a good five minutes. I drummed my fingers on the table.

Meredith avoided my gaze as the returning council members walked past. If she'd tried to save me, it didn't look as if she'd been able to convince anybody.

Genevieve waved a hand in the air. "Enough with the pomp and circumstance. Clearly, Desi's employment with Façade will be terminated, although she can maintain any previous earnings. She will also be sanitized, effective as soon as this meeting concludes." Genevieve glanced down at her watch. "Which I suppose is now. Council dismiss—"

"Wait!" I shot out of my chair. "Wait, look, yes, I did all the stuff and, yes, you should punish me, but before, before I'm . . ." Sanitized. I couldn't say the word. Oh, my gosh, I was seriously going to be sanitized. My magic would be gone . . . and . . . and I wouldn't remember Façade, or any of the princesses I'd subbed for, or Karl. And only half of what I'd shared with Reed. This was really happening. I didn't realize how far I had fallen until I was down in the pit, looking up. "Before I leave. You all should know that when Façade sanitizes subs, they KEEP that magic, and that magic is what Façade is run on, not solely organic magic. And they have makeup that can heal injuries! And—"

"Nonsense," Genevieve said. "Desi, do stop. For your own good, dear."

"No! You made me an ambassador, and I'm going to say what is wrong here. Façade is limiting itself, limiting the help that you can give," I opened my arms to the crowd. "That you *all* can give. And not just to royals, but everyone in the world. You have the power to make an impact."

Two burly guards stepped in from the shadows. One bound my arms, one tried to stick tape on my mouth. Defeated, I collapsed into him, my tears spilling over the guards' hands as he literally shut my mouth.

I couldn't gauge the crowd's reaction because of those stupid masks. The room was quiet, though. Maybe they were thinking about what I had to say, finding truth in my words. Like Reed had.

Reed, who wasn't here. Reed, who had to leave too early and might not have any idea this was happening. Reed, who might be sanitized too.

Genevieve clapped twice. "There will be a reception in Dorshire Hall. Come by, visit with friends, reminisce about the elements that make Façade so great. Thank you for coming. Council dismissed." She pounded a gavel on the table, and the guards began to push me toward the exit.

Lilith grabbed one of their arms. "Wait." Her smile was all sugar, but her voice was pure venom. "Desi, dear. If I didn't have such impeccable breeding, I would spit on you right now. You are worthless, meaningless, and crass. Best of luck back in Hicktown. I'll cherish my memory of this meeting, even if your memory will be gone. Dominick, care to join me at the party?"

Dominick stepped forward, his expression more confused than cruel. "The things you gave up. The glamour, the prestige, the money. It's tragic—there are a million girls out there who would want what you had, and you threw that away. I don't understand you at all."

The rest of the audience shuffled past us as well. Ferdinand tore off his mask, pushed the guard away, and gave me a hug. "You'll always be a princess to me, Miss Bascomb."

I nodded, because obviously I couldn't reply, and the tears went from a trickle to blinding buckets. I would have liked to see Meredith again, but I couldn't find her in the crowd. I wanted her to know that I forgave her for moving Reed, that I understood she was protecting his family. I wanted to thank her for everything, for being my agent.

For being my friend.

But that wasn't going to happen. In a few moments I wouldn't remember her at all. I hardly had the energy to walk out of the room with the guards.

The larger guard gently removed the tape over my mouth and pointed to a wall. "Sit down. Someone will come for you."

Oh, great. I get to cuddle with the bones while I wait for my imminent doom. But this wall was at least stone. I wondered if they would clean me up before I went home again. The hard-packed dirt floor was not going to do much for the gorgeous dress I was wearing.

And . . . since Floressa gave me this dress, I wouldn't remember who I got this dress from. I would go home to that ball, see Kylee, and never be able to tell her that she has magic, because I wouldn't remember my magic. My former magic. We'd go back to worrying about normal things—like Reed moving, although I wouldn't remember why. Maybe I could take up a new hobby, spend time with my family, help my mom get ready for this new baby. I just hoped I didn't suddenly get into wearing makeup. I never wanted to wear makeup again.

I would be fine without Façade. Without Meredith, without my memories, without magic.

Because you can't miss what you never knew you had.

"Darling, why are you sitting on the ground?"

I looked up. Meredith. "The guards told me to."

Meredith offered me a hand and pulled me up. "And you listened? Did those buffoons know you're wearing a Floressa Chase original?"

"I think, at this point, the dress is the least of my worries."

Meredith wrapped her arms around me. "I want you to know you have been the most difficult, headstrong, reckless, ridiculous client I have ever had."

"Thank you."

"No, thank *you*. You're also the bravest, and you've given me the courage to do something I really should have done sooner."

"What's that?"

"Quit."

My jaw dropped. "Meredith, that's just dumb."

"I know. Your stupidity must be contagious."

"But Façade is your life."

"That's *my* problem." Meredith brushed off my dress, avoiding eye contact with me. "I don't want to work at a place that would fire a girl like you. And I do have a rather handsome prince with whom I can live happily ever after. So there is a silver lining for me. Perhaps I'll send you an invite to the wedding."

"Won't matter. I'm not going to remember you, once my memory is washed."

Meredith pursed her lips. "True."

"Can I ask you something that I won't remember in five minutes? What is your magical emotion?"

Meredith smiled. "I wish I could tell you. Over twenty years with this agency, and I still don't know. Many of us still don't know. I was never able to use magic to impact clients like you did. Your ability, your progress, it was all so incredibly rare, Desi."

"Which is why I can't bring myself to destroy that."

Meredith and I turned to see Genevieve standing in the stone doorway. The hall behind her was now empty. She strode into the corridor. "I hate the catacombs. Hate. Let's change the scenery, shall we?" She flicked her wrist and a bubble appeared. She made a face. "Sorry, only traveling bubbles this close to the hall. But it'll be a ten second trip."

We shuffled into the bubble, which barely fit the three of us. I'd assumed Genevieve was taking us straight to the sub-sanitation room, but no. Within seconds we were on top of the roof of the Tour Montparnasse. The air was chilly but fresh, and we had the perfect view of the sun setting just behind the Eiffel Tower.

"Are you dropping me off first?" Meredith asked. "I would like to be there for Desi's sanitation before I pack up my things."

"Don't worry about that just yet. I wanted a chance to

talk to you alone. I'm very curious to know what Desi was thinking during all of this." She gave me an appraising look. "I cannot tell you how interesting it's been watching you over the last few weeks. Every step—you and the Pearson boy figuring out the manuals, your application of job skills to sneak into Façade, the clever story you told your mother when I sent those packages, your resourcefulness in finding the sub—with a little aid from Meredith."

Meredith swallowed but said nothing.

"I'm confused how you saw all that." I said. "I thought—"

"That we weren't watching. Of course. That's what you needed to believe. You got away with everything because I wanted you to get away with everything. Once we knew you and Reed were spending more time together, we tuned into every conversation. That's why I reassigned Meredith and took you on myself. That's why I told Dominick to keep communication brief, to make it seem like I was too busy to care. All those hiccups we created—the Floressa package, the lack of information on your Elsa job—were a test. I wanted to see how quickly you could think in difficult situations. I wanted to see how far you would go with your big plans. And I'll admit, I was quite curious to see what would happen to Caprice, once her magic was restored."

"Nothing," I mumbled. "Her skin tingled. La-di-da."

"Meredith, what did you say her emotion was again?" Genevieve asked.

"Kindness."

"Ah, yes. Well, it seems Caprice made quite a splash at

that wedding. She linked with some important celebrities, and the wheels are set in motion for a charity she'd like to start. Let Them Eat Cake, a program that feeds hungry inner-city children. And her magic, that extra jolt of kindness, was surely her motivation."

"Really?" I couldn't help but beam. "That's amazing. Genevieve, don't you see what good we can do with this power? If we just let the sub hopefuls keep their skills and magic, they can develop those abilities for real-world purposes."

"You have a point," Genevieve said. "You have many good points. And I don't think it would hurt if we explored your philosophies a bit more."

If Meredith's silver lining was her prince, then mine was knowing that I had made some kind of an impact within the agency. "I'm glad you're more open—it'll make the sanitization a little less painful."

Genevieve threw up her hands. "Would you two stop! I'm not going to sanitize you, Desi. And Meredith, I'm not letting you quit."

"What?" Meredith and I said at the same time.

"Well, I obviously had to *say* I was punishing you in front of my council. I would look soft if I didn't sanitize you. But it turns out I *am* soft, and I have an idea that I think will benefit you and Façade both."

"If this is like last time, Genevieve, when you promoted me to Level Three, I won't take your bribe," I said.

"I would like to start a new division at Façade, run by

Meredith and assisted by Desi. I also think Reed Pearson would be a vital asset—"

"Reed? Is Reed okay?" I finally realized that Genevieve was not only aware of my acts of sabotage, but Reed's as well. "You're not going to sanitize him, are you?"

"Reed was never brought before the council. They have no idea that he was involved, and he may continue at Façade. Or he can go into the Organic Magic department, working with his parents in Egypt, and whatever research they do can help your division. You would use magic to help non-royals in whatever capacity you see necessary, as long as those being helped are unaware magic is involved."

Meredith looked like she was about to faint. "You're giving us a new job?"

"Not with Façade. I can't keep you on here after all that has happened. No one here would know what you are doing. But I would fund your research, sort of a charitable donation, and provide a modest stipend for any recruits."

"Recruits? Like Caprice?" I asked.

"If that's where you want to start. But I can't go around handing out magic. What we can do is screen potentials, and send you the ones we feel are better suited to your needs."

"The rejects," I said.

"Call them what you may. Should you find their skills useful, their job would be to positively impact those in need, sort of like what Desi attempted to do while subbing. Their work would be secretive, of course."

"So I'm not getting sanitized or losing my memory,

and Meredith still has a job. We both have jobs."

Genevieve looked at Meredith. "She likes to repeat herself, doesn't she?"

"All the time." Meredith laughed.

I bounced from one foot to the other. Not only did I get to keep my job, but Genevieve was improving it! It was like a dream come true, just not a dream I had even known was possible. "Can we also explore ways to strengthen organic magic? Then you won't have to steal magic anymore."

Genevieve's features hardened. "It would be very difficult to convince the agency to quit that practice altogether. And I believe I'm being very fair in what I offer. We'll continue our magical procedures regardless, and this way, some of the rejected subs will still get to keep their magic, should they choose to continue their employment with your branch."

"Fine, then can *we* be run solely on organic magic?" I asked. "And use us as an experiment? If that works, it would be something for Façade to consider, right?"

"I'll concede that. You never cease to impress me, Desi Bascomb." Genevieve strode across the roof and pushed open the entrance to the emergency stairs. "You two can take a bubble out of here—I'm going to get some exercise on these stairs. And I suppose you can keep your bubble, Desi; no one is going to notice that. And your manual . . . I'll have to figure out how to grant you access on there without Façade being aware of your usage. And I'll have my assistant send out a formal agreement to you this week."

"Just not to my house," I said.

"Yes, no more tricks. You'll be able to do this job without being detected by family or Façade." Genevieve pointed a manicured finger at Meredith. "As for you, we'll hammer out a contract later—I could maybe keep you as an independent consultant, since you weren't fired like Desi. But for now, I think Desi has a ball to get to, and you might want to place a phone call."

"To who?" Meredith asked.

Genevieve's eyes crinkled as she smiled. I might not like how she ran everything at Façade, but we were very lucky to have her support. "Technically, you're no longer a Façade employee. So technically, anything you want to do in your personal life would be your business."

Meredith continued to look confused.

"Your prince, Meredith. Go call your prince." Genevieve gave Meredith a wink and slipped behind the door, leaving Meredith and me alone in the dwindling Paris twilight.

"What just happened?" Meredith asked.

"You just quit Façade," I said. "And I almost got sanitized. And then we got rehired."

"I can't believe it. I get both." Meredith shook her head and whisked out her phone. Her smile was absolutely brilliant. She wasn't doing this with a text this time. Her prince answered on the second ring.

"Roberto," she breathed out. "My answer is yes. Forever and ever. Yes."

Meredith cried and laughed while she flew me home in

her bubble. As soon as she dropped me off, she was zipping right over to see Prince Roberto. And as for me? I didn't know what my life was going to be like from this point on. I knew I would miss subbing—miss my clients, miss being a part of their lives. I would miss Façade—the rich history, the wonderful people who worked there, the mystery of not knowing what each job would bring. No more tiaras, no more princesses, no more glitz and glam.

But on the plus side, I would still be able to see Reed, even after he moved to Egypt. Meredith would be able to guide me as I made this epic leap. I had the opportunity to do the very thing I'd always wanted to do—use magic for good for anyone who needed it, regardless of money or status. I had a future of possibility and excitement with this new organization we would be forming. Genevieve had even given me permission to seek out my own employees.

And I knew exactly who I was hiring first.

Chapter 26

Kylee was already grilling Reed when I got back to the grove, my bubble appearing just behind a tree. He had his hands in his pockets, and he kept flinching as she attacked him with question after question. It was so fun to watch, I didn't interrupt.

"Are you an alien?" she asked. "Cyborg? Unicorn in human form? Warlock? Serial killer."

"I told you, Kylee, I'm just me. And whatever you thought you saw, well, I can promise you won't be seeing it again."

"And what did you do with Desi? Vaporize her? Bite

her? I've heard of invisible werewolves, you know."

Reed rubbed the back of his neck. "I would really like to know where Desi is too. Why don't you go look for her, and I'll wait here in case she comes back."

"No way. I am her *protector*. You go see if she went back to the dance, and *I'll* wait here."

"Kylee, I promise I'm not some psycho from a scary movie."

"That's exactly something a psycho from a scary movie would say."

"Fine. Fine. I'm going to check in at the rink. I have a surprise planned for her. She should be back in a bit, and when she is, and after you've confirmed that she is not an alien clone, can you *please* tell her to come find me?"

"After I check that she has not magically been tampered with."

"Yeah. You do that," Reed muttered.

Kylee sat down on the bench, right next to the hot chocolate I'd set there before I left. I tiptoed behind her, leaned in, and whispered, "Boo!"

Her scream could be heard in Oregon. "DESI BASCOMB! Don't you dare!" She grabbed at her chest, then swallowed me in a hug. "What happened to you? Don't lie. I saw you disappear into . . . I know this sounds stupid, but in a giant—"

"Bubble? Yep."

"For real." Kylee steadied herself on the bench. "So . . . is this what you and Reed were up to? Perfecting your Houdini act? Because he appeared a few seconds after you left. And . . . he's not an evil wizard, right?"

"Kylee, listen to yourself."

"What? I just saw my best friend and the hottest boy in town alternately pop in and out of thin air. What do you want me to think, Desi, IF THAT IS YOUR NAME?"

I moved my hot chocolate and joined Kylee on the bench. "So, you've been asking me for the truth for a really long time, and I'm going to tell you. You probably won't believe it, but I promise you, this is all very real." I took a sip of my still-warm hot chocolate, and started. "So, last June, when I was working at Pets Charming, I made a wish on some magical fish, and a bubble just like the one you saw appeared in my room along with my agent, Meredith, who offered me a job as a magical princess substitute . . ."

I gave her a three minute rundown of the last six months of my life. Kylee didn't interrupt me, just kept nodding like a bobblehead.

" . . . so, yeah. You saw a bubble. And those weird phone things we showed you are our manuals. And you wouldn't have been able to see any of this if you didn't have some MP—Magic Potential."

"Wait—*I'm* magical now?" Kylee rubbed her chin. "Desi, that all sounds so crazy. Like, it's so far out there, I don't know how you could even make it up."

"That's because I'm not making it up."

"And that's why Reed and you are so tight."

I swallowed. "Well, yeah. That's part of the reason."

Kylee played with the fringe on her scarf. "The other part being you both like each other."

"Kylee—"

She held up her hand. "Desi. It's fine. No, seriously, for real this time. You and Reed? I'm okay with it. I had a stupid crush on him, but I can tell it's more for you two. And as your friend, I need you to know I approve and I'm happy and so on. Now. As far as all this magical business goes . . ." Kylee readjusted in her seat. "So when do I get my own bubble? Do I have an agent? Can I borrow your bubble? Can we go wherever we want? Have you met any cute princes? Tell me you can introduce me to a hot prince. Where is this Façade place? And are there any divisions for magical creatures? Because, oh my gosh, Desi, what if we got our own pet unicorn?"

"You should be in shock now." I reached over and felt Kylee's forehead. "Why aren't you in shock? I'm being totally serious about all this. You should be running away and screaming."

Kylee pointed at the spot where my bubble had first appeared. "I just saw you pop out of thin air. And I *am* a musical prodigy, you know, and sometimes when I'm playing my clarinet it feels like there's a . . . power that's helping me perform. Maybe that's magic. And I still sleep with my light on because I'm worried about evil creatures biting me while I sleep. Royal substitutes? Not a stretch."

"The bad news is, I can't offer you a princess job. But

the good news is, I'm helping to start a new agency division. The pay is awful, there is no glamour or perks. We might fail completely, but there will be travel involved as we look for new recruits."

"Like bubbles? Please tell me I get a bubble. And if vampires are real, you better find me a hot one."

"The hottest." I let out a laugh. "I think I'm in shock more then you are. It's such a relief to finally be able to tell you everything."

"And we'll have plenty of time for you to tell me more," Kylee said. "But now you should probably go find Reed. And I will sit here on this very cold bench and digest that I have magical abilities."

"You *will* have magical abilities." I pointed out. "First we have to ignite them, though, and that only comes when you interact with a magical organism. . . . You know what? We'll go over that later. You digest. And here." I tossed her my manual. "Go through the gossip section first. You'll love the insider tips they have on Prince William."

I left Kylee to explore the world of Façade while I tried to find Reed. He wasn't at the skating rink, much to his busy boss's dismay. The decorations committee had sent Celeste over to help, who of course thought *help* was a four-letter word.

I mean, it is a four-letter word. But still.

"Do you know how gross these skates are?" she asked.

"Yeah, yeah, disgusting. Hey, have you seen Reed?"

"He was just here looking for *you*. I saw him go out into

the parking lot. Ooooh, why are you looking for him? I knew you two were in love!"

I ran over to the parking lot, which was filled with cars and festive partygoers in winter coats. I surveyed passing faces until everyone had crammed into the community center and I was left alone. It was cold, and my shoes were not made to walk in snow, and I looked adorable in this peacoat and Floressa Chase original dress, which was not being put to good use searching for Reed.

I heard the jingle bells before I saw them. The horse's hooves clicked against the wet street as the driver pulled closer to the curb in the sleigh. Reed was tucked in under a blanket. He patted the seat next to him. "The driver is named Dave. He does some horticulture work with my dad, so for twenty bucks he agreed to give us our own fifteen-minute sleigh ride." Reed lowered his voice. "He also has incredibly bad hearing, so don't worry about him eavesdropping."

"Hi, Dave!" I called. Dave smiled under his bushy mustache. I hopped up by Reed and settled under the blanket.

"Dave can vouch for me if Kylee starts chasing us, yelling that I'm trying to steal you back to the mother ship."

"She won't. I just told her all about Façade."

Reed frowned. "How did you get away with that?"

"The council can't fire me twice in one day."

"Wow." Reed let out a low whistle. "They really did? I'm sorry I wasn't there. Barrett showed up at the wedding, and my bubble took me right home—I tried to change my location so I could find you, but there was some kind of freeze on the control and I couldn't do anything. I was brought right back here."

"And nothing else happened to you? Sergei or your parents or Genevieve didn't say anything?"

"No. Like I said, I had no clue what was going on. I didn't even get a slap on the wrist."

"About that. Genevieve knows everything we did—she was watching the whole time."

"No way; serious?" Reed's voice cracked. "But then why didn't I have to face the council? They aren't going to call me in, are they?"

"No one else knows you were involved, and Genevieve isn't telling anyone." I shifted in my seat and looked Reed square in the eye. "She offered me a new position, and she wants you to work with me and Façade and your parents, if they want."

Reed leaned back and put his hands behind his head. "I'm in."

"Don't you want to hear what the job is?"

"Another part of having truth as my emotion? Sometimes you don't have to hear the truth—you can feel it. And I trust you so much, Desi, that I am behind you one hundred percent on any new adventure. Plus, we'll still get to see each other, once I move."

I grinned. "Yeah, we will, huh?"

"So I want to hear all about the firing and rehiring, but first I think this is the perfect time to give you your birthday present." Reed reached behind the seat and produced a small box wrapped in gold paper. "I remember you told my parents that it's your birthday tomorrow, and with all the other things going on in your life, you probably haven't thought about it much. And fourteen is a big age."

I peeled back the paper and opened the box. When I saw what was inside, I threw my head back and laughed. A tiara. A real, honest-to-goodness, Celeste-might-wear-this-at-her-pageant TIARA. I pushed back the pink tissue paper and held up my gift in the moonlight. "It's the best present ever."

"I know you were joking when you said the reason you worked at Façade was so you could wear tiaras, but I thought you should still have one of your very own. Besides, you're, uh, more awesome than any princess I've ever met."

I elbowed his side. "Even Floressa Chase?"

"Especially Floressa Chase."

"Oh, come on. I bet you were excited that you got to kiss her."

"No way. I've had to kiss a lot of princesses." Reed reached over and stuck my tiara on my head. "I've kissed Elsa before, too, but you're not acting weird about that."

"What?" I shook my head in disbelief. "Barrett kissed ELSA?"

"No, *Karl* did."

"But you're Barrett."

Reed knocked on my head. "And you're dense. I've subbed for Karl, too. He had me come to Metzahg when he first reunited with Elsa, because he couldn't break up with her on his own. But when I got there, I decided Elsa was just too cool to pass up and told him he should come back and face her. So he did, they kissed, and now they're doing the whole happily-ever-after thing."

"So, you were there?" I asked, misty-eyed. "In the garden?"

"Yeah, I walked around a garden. How'd you know that?"

"I was subbing for Elsa." I was right. Reed was the prince I'd first fallen for. And he was the boy who saved me from the dunk tank. And the sub who'd helped me stand up to Façade. He was everyone. He was everything. "So what does this mean?"

"Desi, I liked you the first time I met you. Yeah, Elsa was really cool that day, so it makes sense if you were her. But honestly? I like you just as you. Not as a princess. Not as a sub." He reached over and took my hand under the blanket. "Just Desi."

And I realized that it didn't matter if part of the time he was Karl—if I kind of had liked Karl—because right now, it was just Reed. Just Reed and me.

"Do you like old movies?" I asked.

"Some of them. I watch them to study acting."

"But you know *Casablanca*."

His face filled with understanding. "Yeah. That was you quoting lines, wasn't it?"

I nodded.

He leaned in and smiled at me, our faces inches apart. "You know what other line I like?"

I shook my head.

"I think this is the beginning of a beautiful friendship."

And then Just Reed leaned over and gave Just Desi a soft, quick kiss. We weren't royals, we weren't actors, and he wasn't saving me from a dunk tank.

And that five-second kiss was my most magical moment yet.

Acknowledgments

Thank you to the following people for being a part of the creation of this book, and part of this whole wacky series. On paper, they're just names, but in life, they are essential to this process and to keeping my brain working.

My agent: Sarah Davies, who is a mentor and a friend. Wow, my little unfinished WIP is now a series. How did that happen? Oh, that's right. I met you.

My editor: Catherine Onder, who is professional and warm, smart and savvy. Your suggestions on this book took things in the directions they were always supposed to go. Thanks for being my guide through Desi's world.

My publisher: Hayley Wagreich, Stephanie Lurie, Hallie Patterson, Dina Sherman, Sara Ortiz, Nellie Kurtzman, Andrew Sansone, Ann Dye, Whitney Manger, Marci Senders, Joann Hill, Marybeth Tregarthen, David Jaffe, Sharon Krinsky, and Emily Schultz. I've harbored a lifelong love of all things Disney, and y'all have turned that love to near obsession. Thanks for adding so much sparkle to this series.

My daughters: Rylee, Talin, and Logan. Do you know why I

wanted to become a writer? Because when Rylee was a baby, I held her in my arms and thought, I want to teach my daughters to go after their dreams. And so, to show you that, I finally went after my writing dream, and it actually came true. But really? My biggest dream fullfilled is each of you. I'm so lucky to be your mom.

My husband: Curry. I love that even though we have such different interests and occupations, we still have a shared love of life. I love when you get defensive about reviews, even though they're totally right, that character was two-dimensional. I love when you give me the standard speech: "Yes, you're going to finish this book. No, I'm sure it's not that bad. Of course you know what you're doing. Fine, I'll get you a Slurpee."

Mostly, I love you.

My parents: Carol and Eric Taylor. Mom, you're crazy, but I love your crazy. And Dad, next book, we're going epic. Like, Middle Earth EPIC. Start inventing a new Elvish language—I'll definitely have some questions. Thank you both for always having the answers.

My child care: Sinclair Johnson. Thanks for the babysitting, wherein no babies were actually sat upon. At least not by you.

Morgan and Kaylee Taylor, Rachel and Spencer Orr, Jan and Berne Leavitt. Since cloning authors is not yet legal, you are the next best thing. You love my kids, and I love you for all of your help. And you love me and they love you and . . . Okay, this is starting to sound like a Barney song.

My writing friends: Holly Westland. Girl, you're good. Thanks for reminding me who Desi is and what she needed to do.

Lisa Schroeder, Rachel Hawkins, Becca Fitzpatrick, and Emily Wing Smith. Sweet snow bunnies, you showed me the light through the darkest plotting moments. Shelli Johannes-Wells, thanks for the bed(s) and the laughs. Irene Latham, your Southern hospitality is unparalleled. And L. K. Madigan, who is no longer with us in body, but always is in spirit, always through her words. I miss you, Lees. Triple L's forever and ever.

My book peeps: thank you especially to Crystal Perkins, a tireless book advocate and dear friend. The staff at The King's English, my local independent bookstore that just happens to be six hours away. Uncle Kyle, for being TKE's very best customer; Uncle Ed, for the Houston support; and my brother Brett, for making that whole standing-in-front-of-an-entire-junior-high nightmare come true, but in a good way. And thank you to the many schools, book clubs, bloggers, and libraries who have championed Desi's story. One of the best things about writing these books is that it gave me the chance to meet you.

My beverage of choice: Diet Pepsi; you're a sweet seductress. Someday I'll quit you. But not until I turn in that next book. . . .

My readers: the fact that you even exist is still a marvel to me. Thank you for your time and support, but most of all, for opening your imagination to this world. These books are done, but the story never ends.

Cue music to *The NeverEnding Story*.

Cue readers to watch the 1984 classic *The NeverEnding Story* so you'll have an idea what I'm talking about. I think it's on sale at Target right now.